Mandie® Mysteries

MANDIE®
AND THE
BURIED
STRANGER

Lois Gladys Leppard

BETHANY HOUSE PUBLISHERS
MINNEAPOLIS, MINNESOTA 55438

Mandie and the Buried Stranger
Copyright © 1999
Lois Gladys Leppard

MANDIE® and SNOWBALL® are registered trademarks
of Lois Gladys Leppard.

Cover illustration by Chris Dyrud

Published by Bethany House Publishers
A Ministry of Bethany Fellowship International
11400 Hampshire Avenue South
Minneapolis, Minnesota 55438
www.bethanyhouse.com

Printed in the United States of America by
Bethany Press International, Minneapolis, Minnesota
55438

Library of Congress Cataloging-in-Publication Data

Leppard, Lois Gladys.
    Mandie and the buried stranger / by Lois Gladys
Leppard.
        p.   cm. — (A Mandie book ; 31)
    Summary: While on spring break from her girls'
school in North Carolina in 1902, fourteen-year-old
Mandie joins her college friend Joe in solving a mystery
in the nearby mountains.
    ISBN 1–55661–384–9
    [1. Mystery and detective stories. 2. North
Carolina Fiction.] I. Title. II. Series: Leppard, Lois
Gladys. Mandie book ; 31.
PZ7.L556Maf   1999
[Fic]—dc21   99–6446
                                                              CIP

18866

For
Lance Wubbels
who has the patience
of Job

Contents

"Difficulties are the stepping stones
to success."

—Anonymous

Chapter 1 / Secret Plans

Mandie and Celia rushed into their room at the Misses Heathwood's School for Girls in Asheville, North Carolina, threw their books on a chair, and danced around the room.

"Two whole weeks of holiday!" Mandie exclaimed.

"Two whole weeks without books!" Celia added.

Spring in 1902 had arrived and all the students were leaving the next day for a two-week break. Mandie Shaw was going home to Franklin, North Carolina, and Celia Hamilton to Richmond, Virginia, but Mandie had other plans for the time.

"I hope Joe Woodard gets home from college by the time I get to his house," Mandie said, calming down to walk around the room. "But, you know, New Orleans is such a long way off. I don't know why he couldn't have found a college nearer home."

"Oh, Mandie, you do know," Celia said, frowning as she stood still to look at her friend. "The college down there let him in early, and it also teaches what Joe needs to learn to become a lawyer."

"Yes, I know," Mandie said with a sigh, stopping to pick up her books.

"How will you know whether he is home or not?" Celia asked.

Mandie laid her books on the desk in their room and replied, "Well, you see, I have to go home first, and then Uncle John will take me to the Woodards' house. I'm sure Uncle John will know. Dr. Woodard will probably send him a message. I wish you could go with me."

"Not this time. I have to go home," Celia told her, sitting down in the chair with her books. "But I promise I will go to your house when school is out for the summer." She pushed back her long, curly auburn hair as she looked at Mandie.

"I hope Jonathan will be able to come down from New York," Mandie said. "And that Sallie can join us, too. We're going to have an exciting summer if we can all get together. I know for sure Joe will be around."

"Do you think Jonathan's father will come down with him? Will your grandmother be at your house then?" Celia asked.

Mandie sat on the window seat and smiled as she said, "I have no idea. But I do know my grandmother doesn't like Jonathan Guyer's father for some reason or other. One of these days I'm going to find out why."

"I hope you do because I'd like to know, too," Celia said, grinning at her friend.

Suddenly there was a loud banging noise and

then a sharp hissing sound. Both girls jumped up, startled.

"Oh shucks!" Mandie said with a frown as she looked around the room. "That was that crazy old radiator acting up!"

"Sure it was," Celia agreed. "I'll just never get used to that noise."

"Me either," Mandie agreed. "But you've got to admit our room has been warmer since we came back from Christmas holidays and the furnace had been installed. If it just wouldn't make that terrible noise."

"I know, but I still think I would rather have kept the fire in the fireplace," Celia said. She looked overhead to a single light bulb hanging from the ceiling. "And that stupid way of having a light is dumb. Why couldn't they wire the room so we could have some electric lights on the walls down here or lamps or something instead of sticking the light all the way up to the ceiling?"

Mandie grinned mischievously at her friend and said, "We should have been here while they were working on all this and told them how we wanted everything. At least Miss Prudence has let us keep our oil lamps in our rooms."

"Thank goodness," Celia said. "Why, I can't even see good enough to read by that light bulb up there. You know that."

"Yes, and I think that's why we are allowed to keep our lamps," Mandie agreed. "I suppose the next thing will be installing a telephone here in the school, but that will probably be put in Miss Prudence's office downstairs so they won't bother us with that."

"Maybe they can do that while we're on break

the next two weeks," Celia said.

"Right," Mandie agreed as she jumped up. "Right now I'm going to pack my things so I'll be ready when Grandmother sends Ben for me in the morning."

After an evening of packing and talking, the girls were up early the next morning. The furnace acted like an alarm clock. When Uncle Cal, the janitor, built up the fire downstairs in the furnace, the heat would rise to the rooms upstairs, and the radiators would start banging and hissing. This usually happened around five o'clock every morning. Mandie and Celia would stay snuggled under the quilts for about thirty minutes after this started, and by that time their room would be warm enough for them to step down on the cold floor and get dressed. But they were in a hurry this particular morning and didn't wait for the temperature to rise in their room.

"You know even though we're in the first sitting for breakfast at seven-thirty, we still have to eat before we can leave," Mandie reminded her friend as she quickly pulled on a navy dress with white lace trimming. "And that means we have to stay here until at least eight-thirty. So I don't know why we got up so early."

"Oh, Mandie, I couldn't have slept another wink," Celia replied. She was buttoning up the front of her dark brown dress. "I'm as anxious as you are to get home. So just as soon as Aunt Rebecca gets here, I'll get the train with her back to Richmond."

"And Ben will probably be waiting for me as soon as we have breakfast," Mandie said, quickly brushing her long blond hair. "And Grandmother and I will be leaving on the train to Franklin."

Mandie's grandmother, Mrs. Taft, lived in Asheville, and Ben was her driver. She always sent him in the rig to pick Mandie up from school when Mandie was coming to visit her. And sometimes Mrs. Taft kept Snowball, Mandie's cat, because Mandie boarded at the school and there had to be a special reason for him to be allowed to stay at the school, such as the time a mouse got in Mandie's and Celia's room while the workmen were boring holes to install the furnace and the electrical wiring.

"I know Snowball will be glad to see you," Celia remarked as she, too, began brushing her hair. "He's been at your grandmother's ever since we came back from the Christmas holidays, and you haven't been to her house since then."

"And I'll be glad to see Joe Woodard to find out what he was trying to tell me when he left on the train to go to college and we said good-bye at the first of the year. He was yelling something at me out the train window when it pulled out of the station, and he promised to write. The only thing I've heard from him was the note the other day saying he would be home for the spring holidays," Mandie said with a frown.

"He's probably been awfully busy getting settled into college," Celia said. She tied her hair back with a ribbon to match her dress.

"Anyhow, I'll find out what it was just as soon as I see him, which shouldn't be too much longer," Mandie replied, turning in front of the full-length mirror to inspect her dress. "Let's go downstairs and see if anyone else is up. That way we'll be first in line for breakfast."

When Mandie and Celia got down to the main hallway, they were surprised to see other students waiting around. Everyone seemed in a hurry to leave school. Even Miss Prudence, the head school-mistress, who presided over the first sitting for breakfast, seemed in a hurry to get the pupils on their way. It was the shortest meal Mandie had ever sat through at the school.

When Mandie and Celia left the dining room, they glanced out the front door.

"Ben is already out there!" Mandie exclaimed, going to open the door.

"Celia!" someone called from behind them, and the two girls turned around to find Celia's aunt Rebecca waiting for them in the little alcove at the front window. "The train was early," the lady said, rising to come toward them.

"Oh, Aunt Rebecca, I'm so glad. Maybe the train home will be early, too," Celia said, going to embrace her aunt.

"I'm glad to see you, Aunt Rebecca," Mandie greeted the woman and was immediately hugged by her. Even though she was no kin to Mandie, Mandie called her "Aunt Rebecca" with her permission, since Mandie had no aunts of her own.

"I hope you have a nice journey home, dear," Aunt Rebecca told her.

"Thank you," Mandie replied. "Ben is out there waiting, so I'll let him know he can get my trunk now. See y'all in two weeks."

"Have fun," Celia called to her as Mandie went out the front door to speak to Ben.

When Mandie got to her grandmother's house, and the maid opened the door, Snowball came rushing out and went wild rubbing around Mandie's ankles. She stooped and picked him up. "So you are glad to see me," Mandie told him as she rubbed her cheek on his soft white fur.

"Amanda, come on in," Mrs. Taft called from down the hallway. "We'll be leaving soon."

Mandie set Snowball down and hurried to embrace her grandmother. Snowball ran off down the hallway. "I haven't seen you since we came back to Asheville. We never stay apart that long at one time."

"I know, dear," Mrs. Taft said, squeezing Mandie's shoulders. "We're going to have to work out our schedules so we have more time together. Now take off your coat and tam, and we'll sit by the fire in the parlor until it's time to leave."

Mandie hung her coat and tam on the hall tree and followed her grandmother into the parlor. She saw the fire burning brightly in the fireplace and asked, "Oh, Grandmother, you haven't had one of those furnaces put in your house yet?"

As they sat down, Mrs. Taft smiled and replied, "Oh yes, dear, we do have what they call central heat now, but I don't intend doing away with my fires in the fireplaces all the time."

Mandie quickly looked around the room and spotted a radiator beneath the windows to the front porch in the room. "I see," she said. "Do your radiators make all that racket like the ones at school? Celia and I always think something is blowing up when it happens."

Mrs. Taft laughed and replied, "They do make some noise, but once you learn how to stoke them, they are not so bad. Evidently Uncle Cal at the school isn't keeping them going evenly."

"I suppose as soon as it gets warm weather, Miss Prudence will have them all turned off," Mandie said with a big sigh. Then she changed the subject. "Are you going to stay at our house until it's time for me to come back to school?"

"I'm not certain at the moment," Mrs. Taft told her. "But I probably will. Hilda is still at the Mannings' house, and they have been asking if they can keep her. They want to give her a home."

"Hilda live with the Mannings?" Mandie questioned. "Well, I suppose that would be all right, provided we could see her now and then."

"Of course, that would be understood," Mrs. Taft said. "You know, Hilda is much better off with them because they have that daughter who lives at home. She doesn't go off to school out of town like you do. And Hilda seems to get along very well with the daughter."

"Have you already promised them Hilda could live with them?" Mandie asked.

Mandie and Celia had found Hilda hiding in their schoolhouse and had rescued her and brought her home to Mrs. Taft. Therefore, Mandie felt a close connection with the girl, even though Hilda didn't seem to know how to talk very well and had some kind of handicap for learning.

"No, dear, I just told them we would discuss it later, when you and I come back to Asheville," Mrs. Taft said.

The maid came into the parlor just then with a tray and put it on the table next to Mrs. Taft. Mandie spotted sweet rolls on it alongside the coffeepot.

"Now let's have a little refreshment before we board that noisy, dirty old train," Mrs. Taft told Mandie, picking up the cup of coffee the maid had poured for her.

Mandie took the other cup of coffee and moved closer to the table to look over the fancy delicacies on the tray, but especially the sweet rolls.

"We made them especially for you, Missy 'Manda," Ella, the maid, told her with a big grin as she watched.

"Oh, thank you," Mandie said, smiling up at the girl as she quickly took one of the rolls on a little plate from the tray. She took a big bite and spoke with her mouth full. "Umm! Good!"

"Thank you, Ella, that will be all for now," Mrs. Taft dismissed the maid, who quickly left the room. Then turning to Mandie, Mrs. Taft asked, "Amanda, are you not learning anything at that school? You know you shouldn't talk with food in your mouth."

Mandie quickly swallowed and replied, "I know. I'm sorry, Grandmother. I suppose Miss Prudence is so strict on us that I have to loosen up when I get away from her."

"But that is a big mistake, Amanda," Mrs. Taft said. "If you don't mind your p's and q's all the time, you will forget sometime and make a big blunder, like, uh . . ." She tried to think of an example.

"Like visiting with the President of the United States?" Mandie quickly finished for her. "Yes, President McKinley was so nice and so friendly. It was hard to remember to be on my best behavior, but I don't believe I made a real big mistake. I tried hard."

"No, as I remember, you did very well," Mrs. Taft agreed. "Now, have you thought about what you would like to do this summer? We went to Europe last summer, but we could always go back if you're interested."

Mandie quickly replied, "Oh no, Grandmother, I don't want to go anywhere. I mean, not Europe at least. I would like to stay home this summer, I think."

Mrs. Taft quickly looked at her and asked, "Have you lost all interest in seeing the world? You know I would like to show you everything."

"No, it isn't that, Grandmother," Mandie said, not daring to look at her grandmother as she tried to think of some excuse. "I think my friends will all visit after school is out—Celia, Sallie, Jonathan, and Joe, that is."

"I see," Mrs. Taft said, watching her closely. "Then perhaps they would like to go with you and me somewhere, some special place that you'd like to visit."

Mandie took a deep breath, set down her coffee cup, and said, "I just don't know. I'd have to ask them. You see, we had all talked about this at Christmastime and decided we would visit all our homes. You know, we would all go to Joe's, Sallie's, Jonathan's, and Celia's, and they would come to my house first."

"Now, that sounds like a weary summer, running from Franklin, to Charley Gap, to Deep Creek, to Richmond, and New York. Why, you'd be spending most of your time traveling all that distance," Mrs. Taft said. "Why don't you just ask all your friends to come along with you and me, and we'll go wherever you want."

"Thank you, Grandmother," Mandie said, hoping her grandmother would change the subject. She didn't want her to know that she would be running off to Joe's house as soon as Uncle John would take her. "I'll ask everyone."

"Now that we have that settled, I believe we'd better get ready to go to the depot," Mrs. Taft said, rising from her chair.

Oh goodness, Mandie thought. Her grandmother

seemed to think she had agreed to take her friends and go with her someplace. And she didn't believe her friends would go along with that. They all wanted to escape adult supervision for the summer. They were getting too old to tag along with parents and grandparents all the time. How was she ever going to get out of this?

"Come along, Amanda," Mrs. Taft said as she left the room.

"Yes, ma'am, I'm coming," Mandie said, following her out the door.

When they arrived at the depot, the train came in on time. After they got aboard, Mandie held Snowball in her lap and was thankful to see that her grandmother intended to doze off during the trip. That way she wouldn't have to discuss the possibility of a summer journey. But Mandie soon found herself getting sleepy. She wrapped Snowball's red leash around her wrist and slid down in her seat to get comfortable.

The next thing Mandie knew the conductor was calling, "Franklin! Franklin!" She quickly straightened up to see her grandmother smoothing her skirt and preparing to stand up.

"Home!" Mandie exclaimed, looking out the window. There was Uncle John waiting for them on the platform. Holding securely to the white cat, she followed her grandmother out of the train.

Uncle John Shaw greeted Mrs. Taft, "So glad you could come with Mandie."

"Of course," Mrs. Taft replied.

Then the tall man bent down to embrace Mandie and the white kitten she was holding. "I'm glad you're home, my little blue eyes."

"So am I, Uncle John," Mandie replied, putting

an arm around his neck. Then looking up at him, she asked, "Uncle John, do you have any messages for me?"

"Messages for you?" John Shaw asked with a puzzled expression as he straightened up.

Mandie noticed that her grandmother had also turned to listen as they left the platform of the depot. "You know, any word from anyone I know?" she tried to explain without really explaining.

"Oh, I see," John Shaw said, winking at her. "No, I don't believe I have heard anything from any of your friends."

Mandie frowned, thinking to herself that he must have understood that she was really asking if he had heard whether Joe was home or not. Somehow she just didn't want her grandmother to know, mainly because her grandmother was trying to arrange her summer vacation.

Uncle John had come in the rig, and Jason Bond was with him. Mr. Bond was already inside the depot getting their luggage.

"I'll be right back. I need to help Jason Bond with the luggage," John Shaw told Mrs. Taft as he helped her board the rig.

Mandie jumped up and sat on the backseat. Snowball was trying to get away from her, but she held firmly to his leash.

When they got to the house, all the servants were waiting to greet her in the hallway. To Mandie they were all a part of her family and she loved them all—Aunt Lou, Liza, Jenny, and Abraham. And they always seemed happy when Mandie came home.

After removing her coat and tam and hanging them on the hall tree, Mandie hugged every one of the servants. Then she finally got to the parlor, where her mother was sitting and where her grandmother had already sat down.

"I'm glad you're home, dear," her mother, Elizabeth Shaw, told her as they embraced.

"Me too," Mandie said with a big smile.

Her mother had married Mandie's uncle John Shaw after Mandie's father had died, and Mandie was so grateful to have a real home. She sat down on a stool by the fire in the fireplace.

"I was just asking Amanda what she would like to do this summer," Mrs. Taft said to her daughter. "Perhaps you and John could join us this summer for a trip somewhere."

Oh goodness, why doesn't Grandmother forget about that journey she wants to take this summer? Mandie thought to herself.

"I'm not sure yet what our plans are, but John and I can discuss it," Elizabeth replied.

At that moment Mandie happened to look at the doorway and saw Liza, the young maid, standing there, motioning to her. Mandie quickly glanced at her mother and grandmother and managed to get up and go out to the hallway without being noticed.

"Missy 'Manda, you got a letter," Liza whispered.

"A letter? Where is it?" Mandie asked in surprise.

"Over dere in dat plate whut holds de mail," Liza replied, pointing to the table in the hallway.

Mandie rushed over to look. Sure enough, there was a small white envelope addressed to her, and, if she wasn't terribly mistaken, the handwriting belonged to Joe. She snatched it up and ran to sit on the bottom step of the huge staircase in the main hallway. Liza silently followed, almost as excited as Mandie.

Mandie tore the envelope open and glanced at the one sheet of paper with only three lines of writing on it. "I will be home by the time you get this. Are you coming here, or am I coming there?" It was signed, "Joe."

"From Doctuh son, ain't it?" Liza said, excitedly dancing around the hallway.

"Yes, it is, Liza, and he's already home from school," Mandie replied as she tried to decide what to do next. She couldn't very well run off as soon as she arrived home, but, on the other hand, she wanted to go to the Woodards' instead of having Joe come to her house. That was what they had been planning, anyway.

"He not comin' heah?" Liza asked as she came to a stop by Mandie.

"No, I don't think so," Mandie said thoughtfully. Uncle John had previously promised her he would take her to the Woodards, so that was what she was going to do.

"Den you gwine out dere?" Liza asked.

"Yes, I am," Mandie replied.

"Right now?" Liza asked.

Mandie smiled at her friend and said, "No, not right now, Liza. I just got home. I have to stay a little while, and then I'll go."

"Don't tell Missy Polly, 'cuz she be wantin' to go, too," Liza warned her.

"Polly wants to go to Joe's house?" Mandie asked as she stood up and carefully folded the letter and put it in her pocket.

"Dat whut she dun tole huh cook, and huh cook dun tole me dat she be wantin' to do sumpin' dis heah summer, so she might be gwine somewhere wid you," Liza explained.

"Oh no, Liza, don't let her know anything," Mandie said quickly. "She got home yesterday, didn't she, because she left school one day early?"

"Dat's right," Liza said. "Don't you worry none now, Missy 'Manda. I won't be tellin' huh nuthin', nuthin' a-tall."

Polly Cornwallis lived next door to Mandie, and their mothers were good friends. But Polly was always butting into things and inviting herself. And she was especially interested in Joe. That was another reason Mandie decided she didn't want Joe to come to her house. Polly would find out and be right underfoot the whole time.

"Thanks for telling me, Liza," Mandie said. "I'll let you know when I'm going to Joe's."

As she went back toward the parlor, Mandie wondered when she would be able to leave, but the sooner the better. She wanted to know what Joe had been trying to tell her out of the train window when he had gone away to school.

Chapter 2 / More Plans

Mandie was pleasantly surprised the next morning when Uncle John asked at the breakfast table, "When are you planning to go to the Woodards'? I have some business I'd like to attend to in Asheville as soon as possible. So if we could go to the Woodards' tomorrow after church, I could go on to Asheville from there, and then come back to get you whenever you are ready to return home. What do you think?"

Mandie smiled and replied as she laid down her fork, "Oh, Uncle John, that would be just fine."

"Amanda," her mother said from the end of the huge table. "You just got home, and you are going away?"

"I'm sorry, Mother," Mandie quickly told her. "But if I could go to the Woodards' with Uncle John tomorrow, I could come back in a few days . . . whenever he could get me."

John Shaw looked at his wife from the head of

the table and said, "If you don't want us to do this, we can postpone her visit a few days. But you know I do have to go to Asheville and see our lawyer."

"Well, maybe it would work out better the way you've planned it," Elizabeth slowly agreed. "So just go ahead tomorrow." Turning to Mandie, she said, "Just don't plan on staying at the Woodards' the whole two weeks you will be out of school. You will come home when your uncle concludes his business and comes back for you."

"Yes, ma'am," Mandie quickly agreed. "Thank you, Mother, for letting me go."

"Don't forget about asking Joe if he would be interested in going with you and your other friends someplace this summer," Mrs. Taft reminded Mandie. "I'll foot the bill, and y'all just let me know where you want to go."

"Yes, ma'am, I'll ask Joe," Mandie promised, but she wished her grandmother would stop insisting they go on a trip with her in the summer. She was sure her friends wouldn't agree to it. At least they'd better not.

It turned out to be a long day. Mandie kept watching the clock and wishing the time away so Sunday would come and she would be on her way to Joe's. She was so eager to find out what Joe had been trying to tell her from the train. She also wanted to know how Joe liked college, because she would be going away to a college somewhere in a couple of years and had no idea what to expect.

But the time did finally arrive when John Shaw was urging her to hurry up and get in the buggy. He wanted to get to the Woodards' before dark, and it was a mountainous road. Mandie threw a small valise with a change of clothes in it into the back of the buggy and kissed her mother good-bye.

"I won't be gone long, just until Uncle John can bring me back, Mother," Mandie promised.

"Give my regards to Mrs. Woodard, dear," Elizabeth said, embracing her daughter.

Then Mrs. Taft stepped forward to give Mandie a big hug as she said, "Yes, do hurry back and let me know what Joe has to say about traveling somewhere this summer, dear."

"Yes, ma'am," Mandie said, then she quickly turned to jump up on the step and into the buggy, where Uncle John was waiting impatiently.

As they traveled along the bumpy dirt road, Mandie decided to take Uncle John into her confidence. She thought he would understand.

"Uncle John, I have a problem," Mandie began, looking up at Uncle John's brown eyes as he turned to her.

"You do?" he said with a smile. "Why, that's terrible."

"Oh, Uncle John, this is serious," Mandie said without smiling.

"All right, little blue eyes, what is it?" he asked as he drove the buggy on.

"First of all, I really love Grandmother," Mandie began slowly. "But you know how she is, always wanting to be in charge of everything and all that." She paused for his answer.

"I sure do," John Shaw said with a little laugh. "She is one independent lady." Bending toward Mandie, he added in a loud whisper, "And I'm so thankful her daughter is not like that at all."

"I know. Mother lets people just run over her sometimes, and I wish she wouldn't," Mandie said.

"Now, hold on there, little blue eyes. You know

I'd never run things over your mother. I love her too much. After all, I did wait all those years to marry her, while your father was living," John Shaw tried to explain.

But that statement caused tears to well up in Mandie's eyes. "I don't think you ought to say such things," she said with a shaky voice. "I loved my father so much."

John Shaw reached to squeeze Mandie's hand. "I'm sorry, dear," he said. "I didn't say things exactly the right way. I just wanted you to know how much I do love your mother."

Mandie quickly wiped a tear from her cheek and said, "That's all right, Uncle John." She took a deep breath and continued. "But Grandmother always wants to run everything, and now she's trying to plan my summer for me."

John Shaw looked at her again, smiled, and said, "Well, now, exactly what is it she's planning?"

"Nothing in particular yet," Mandie told him. "She wants me to tell her where I'd like to go this summer, and she'll take me, and my friends, too, if they want to go. But that's not what my friends and I are planning at all."

"I understand what you mean," he replied. "Would you mind telling me what you and your friends are planning for the summer?"

"Well, you see, when everyone was at our house at Christmastime, we decided we would visit everyone's house. Everyone will come to our house first—that is, Jonathan, Joe, Sallie, and Celia. And then we'll all go together and visit Joe's house, Sallie's house, Celia's house, and Jonathan's in New York," Mandie explained, hoping he would understand and help her out on these plans.

"And your grandmother is wanting to take all of you with her somewhere? Is that it?" John Shaw asked.

"Yes, sir," Mandie agreed. "We just want to get away from the adults and do some things on our own for a change."

"Oh, but you all can't travel around the country like that without an adult along, dear," John Shaw told her.

"Why couldn't we?" Mandie asked in surprise.

"In the first place, it wouldn't be safe, running all over everywhere, especially to New York, and it wouldn't be proper, either, you know," he explained.

"But, Uncle John, we don't want Grandmother to go with us," Mandie protested. She had brought Snowball with her, and he woke up in her lap and tried to get down. Holding on to his leash, she said, "Be still, Snowball."

"Perhaps someone else could go with y'all," John Shaw suggested.

"But who? All the grown-ups are always so busy with their own business," Mandie replied. She patted Snowball's head as he curled back up in her lap.

John Shaw smiled at her and asked, "Would you like me to ask your mother if we could join y'all on this adventure? That is, if you want us along."

Mandie became excited and quickly said, "That would be wonderful! Do you think Mother would agree? Do you, Uncle John? Without Grandmother, that is?"

"We won't know until we ask her," he said. "Therefore, we'll find out just as soon as we get back home."

"But how are we going to get around Grand-mother?" Mandie asked.

"You leave that to me. I'll figure out something," John Shaw assured her as he drove on down the rutty road.

Mandie was overjoyed by Uncle John's sugges-tion. She could hardly wait to share it with Joe.

By the time they reached the Woodards' house, the sun had slipped behind the Nantahala Mountain and the spring air had become chilly. Mandie looked forward to the warmth of the fire she knew would be in the Woodards' parlor fireplace. But when they ar-rived, Joe was not home.

"Come in, come in," Mrs. Woodard greeted them at the door. Mr. Miller had taken John Shaw's buggy and horse to the barn when they pulled up at the back door, and he would bring their bags to the house.

"I've brought Amanda here," John Shaw said with a teasing grin as he looked at Mandie. "Seems she must have secrets to share with Joe."

"Yes, those two are always having secrets," Mrs. Woodard agreed, smiling at Mandie as she closed the door. "Take off your coats."

Mandie was holding Snowball in her arms, and she said to Mrs. Woodard, "I hope you don't mind if I brought Snowball."

"Of course not. I know that cat goes wherever you go," Mrs. Woodard replied. "Just put him down. He'll be all right. I'm sure he'll find the fire in the parlor fireplace."

Mandie stooped to set Snowball down, and as she removed her coat she saw him run directly toward the parlor.

John Shaw and Mandie hung their coats and

hats on the hall tree and followed Mrs. Woodard into the parlor. Mandie looked around. There was no one else there. She went over to sit on a low stool by the fireplace, where Snowball was already curling up on the rug.

"Is Dr. Woodard home?" John Shaw asked as he and Mrs. Woodard sat down.

"No, he and Joe took some hot soup over to old Mrs. Donohue, who is ailing with a cold," Mrs. Woodard replied. "But they'll be back any minute now. We knew y'all would be here sometime during the school holidays, and we figured it would be today since Joe said he had sent Amanda a note saying he would be home."

"I've only come to leave Amanda here. I'll be going on to Asheville early tomorrow morning to take care of some business, and I'll be back for her in a day or two or so," John Shaw explained.

"A day or two?" Mrs. Woodard questioned him. "I believe Joe was hoping Amanda could stay longer than that. He is so excited about college, and it will probably take him days to tell her all about it."

"And I'm anxious to hear all about it," Mandie spoke up.

"But you know, Mrs. Woodard, Amanda has only two weeks out from school, and her mother wants to spend some time with her," John Shaw explained.

"Yes, I understand," Mrs. Woodard agreed.

Mandie was thinking all this time, *Just a day or two?* She thought she would have at least a few days with Joe, but she realized she would have to return home with Uncle John when he came back from Asheville. At least summer vacation was not far off.

At that moment Snowball suddenly stood up and growled, his fur standing up. And Mandie heard a horse outside.

As Mrs. Woodard and Uncle John both looked at the strange behavior of the cat, Mandie explained with a smile, "Joe is back. He must have Samantha with him, and Snowball knows it. He doesn't like Joe's dog."

Mrs. Woodard smiled at her and agreed. "Joe did take Samantha with him and his father, but he won't be bringing her in the house. So don't worry about Snowball."

Mandie heard the back door open and close, then the sound of Joe and his father talking as they came down the hallway. They stopped in the doorway to the parlor as they removed their coats and hats.

Mandie stood up with a big smile and said, "Joe! You did make it home from college way down yonder in New Orleans, after all."

"I sure did!" Joe replied with a grin, rushing back to hang up his coat and hat.

"Good to see you, John, and you, too, Miss Amanda," Dr. Woodard said as he left his coat and hat on the hall tree and came into the parlor. He sat down in a chair near John Shaw.

"Nice to visit you again," John Shaw agreed.

Joe rushed into the parlor and went to sit on the rug by the stool where Mandie had sat back down. He held out his hands toward the fire. "Cold outside for March, almost April at that," he said. "The fire sure feels good after living with those radiators at college." Snowball lay back down and curled up at his feet as Joe rubbed his head.

Mandie grinned and said, "So you have radiators, too! They finally got them in our school, and the only good thing about them is that our room is so much warmer. They make noises when Celia and I are not expecting it, and it causes us to jump. We also got electricity with a light bulb hanging from the ceiling, but Miss Prudence let us keep our oil lamps because we couldn't see to read very well by that silly light bulb. Do you have electricity at the college?" She could feel herself getting all wound up and excited now that Joe was here. Somehow she had become shy around her old friend and she didn't understand why.

Joe smiled and replied, "Yes, those radiators are always jumping up and down, and we do have electricity. But we have lights lower down on the walls in brackets, sort of like those candles in the brackets in your uncle's office room."

"Maybe Miss Prudence will get that kind since she knows we can't see very well with those light bulbs overhead," Mandie said, shifting her eyes instead of looking directly at Joe. She fidgeted with her skirt, smoothing it out.

"I hope so. Electricity is no good if you can't see by it," Joe declared. Then he lowered his voice as he said, "I'm glad you came. I have lots of things to tell you."

"I'm glad I could come, too, because I want to know all about your college," Mandie replied. "Also, we need to talk about this summer. Remember you, Sallie, Jonathan, and I talked about getting together and visiting all our houses and Celia's?"

Joe sighed and said, "I remember, but you know what? I may have to stay in school all summer to get caught up to be registered as a full-time student in the fall. The subjects aren't that hard. It's just that there is so much that Mr. Tallant didn't teach and that I need as a basic foundation."

"Oh, Joe, no!" Mandie exclaimed. "You've got to come home this summer. You see, Grandmother is trying to arrange everything." She explained to Joe what she meant. "But I'm hoping my mother and Uncle John will travel around with us this summer."

"That would be nice," Joe said. "But your uncle is right. We would need an adult with us."

Mandie was anxious to ask Joe what he had been trying to tell her from the train that day, but she thought it might be something she didn't want to discuss right now within hearing of the adults.

"How long have you been home?" Mandie asked.

"I got home Friday," Joe said. "And Uncle Ned came by Friday. He said Sallie is helping Mr. O'Neal with the Cherokee school. So I thought maybe we could go see them while you're here."

Mandie explained that Uncle John would be returning in a day or two or maybe three to take her home. "So I won't have a lot of time here," Mandie said regretfully.

"I was hoping you could stay longer than that," Joe said in a disappointed voice. Then he added, "But we could still go visit Sallie. We'd have time for that."

"All right," Mandie agreed. "Now tell me about your college."

"Well, it has several huge brick buildings on the grounds," Joe explained. "The boys live in one of them. There are a few girl students, but they have to live out in town in rooms, or whatever. I've met several nice fellows, but I haven't had time to really get acquainted because I've been studying day and night to catch up to meet the school's requirements for entrance."

"Have you met any of the girls?" Mandie asked teasingly.

Joe hesitated a moment and then, shrugging his shoulders, replied, "Well, I've seen some girls around, but they haven't been in any of the classes I'm taking."

"Are there any pretty ones?" Mandie wanted to know. She smiled at Joe.

"Pretty ones?" Joe questioned.

"Yes, pretty girls, Joe, pretty girls," Mandie told him with a big grin.

"Pretty girls?" Joe repeated. Then looking directly at Mandie, he said, "Oh yes, there is this beautiful blue-eyed blond, short, sorta thin, who loves to solve mysteries. I believe her name is Mandie."

Mandie laughed out loud. "Oh, Joe! I'm talking about girls at your college, but if you don't want to tell me, then what about the boys? Are there any handsome boys in your classes?"

"I suppose you would call some of them handsome," Joe said with a grin. "But I don't intend introducing you to them to see what you think."

"But if I come down to visit you, I can see for myself," Mandie reminded him.

Joe became solemn as he looked at Mandie and said, "Yes, you could see for yourself. But I hope you don't ever meet another fellow that you get too interested in, because I'm reminding you right here and now that I am still planning on marrying you when we finish growing up, Mandie Shaw."

Mandie felt herself blush, and she wouldn't meet Joe's brown eyes as he looked at her. What was this strange feeling she was having that made her feel so shy around her old friend Joe? She didn't understand what had gotten into her.

"That's a long time in the future, when we have grown up, that is," Mandie reminded him. She cleared her throat and asked, "Now, when are we going to see Sallie?"

"I suppose we'd better go tomorrow morning, since you don't have long to stay here," Joe replied. "But it won't do you any good to change the subject, Mandie Shaw, because in no time flat we'll be all grown up one of these days."

Mandie glanced at the adults who were carrying on their own conversation. She was afraid one of them might have overheard Joe's conversation with her. But if they had, no one showed it.

Mandie changed the subject. "I suppose one of these days my mother will pick out a college somewhere for me to go to in a couple of years," she said.

"Come to mine. We'd have two years there to track down all those mysteries in New Orleans, and it is a very mysterious place, very interesting and very old," Joe said. "There's no telling what kind of a mystery we might run across."

"But it's also very far away from my home," Mandie reminded him.

"Any college you go to will be a long way from home," Joe reminded her. "Just hope your mother doesn't pick one way up north someplace, like New York. That place is too big, and there are too many people there."

"I imagine I'll have a little say-so about where

I'm going to college," Mandie told him. "Uncle John would help me out on that with Mother."

"I know," Joe teased. "Your uncle has you spoiled rotten."

Mandie quickly said, "I'm no more rotten than you are, Joe Woodard!" She felt her old, comfortable friendship with Joe returning as the shyness went away.

At that moment Mrs. Miller, who worked for the Woodards and lived with her husband in a cabin on the Woodard property, came to the parlor doorway. Mrs. Woodard saw her and asked, "You have everything on the table?"

"Yes, ma'am," Mrs. Miller told her. "All ready to eat."

"Thank you, Mrs. Miller. We'll be right in," Mrs. Woodard replied.

Mrs. Miller went back down the hallway. Mrs. Woodard rose and said, "I imagine everyone is hungry now. And we have plenty of food on the table. So let's move on into the dining room."

"I'm not rotten," Joe said under his breath as everyone went into the hallway. He grinned down at Mandie.

"We will continue this conversation later," Mandie promised as they followed the adults into the dining room and were seated at the table next to each other.

John Shaw spoke from down the other side of the table, "Amanda, I will be leaving early in the morning, probably before you get up, but please remember I will be back for you most likely on Wednesday, or Thursday at the latest."

"Yes, sir, I'll remember," Mandie promised. "Will you be staying in Asheville until then?"

"Your grandmother has graciously invited me to stay at her house while I attend to my business there, so, yes, I'll be in Asheville. My lawyer is there, and I'll be spending some time with him, going over legal transactions and such," John Shaw explained. "But you just be sure you are here when I return. I don't want to have to run all over the countryside looking for you." He smiled at her.

"I'll be here, Uncle John," Mandie promised.

Joe looked at Mandie, grinned, and said, "I won't let her run off somewhere chasing a mystery."

"That's impossible, because you always go along on the mystery with me when I find one," Mandie reminded him with a big smile.

"In that case we'd better see that you and Miss Amanda are both here," Dr. Woodard told his son.

"And Snowball," Mrs. Woodard added. "Y'all know how he likes to run away."

"And Snowball," John Shaw agreed.

As the adults became engaged in their own conversation, Mandie whispered to Joe, "Do you suppose it's all right if we go see Sallie? That's a long way off."

"Oh sure," Joe said. "I'll let my mother know in the morning where we are going. I don't think your uncle expects you to just sit here and not do anything."

"All right, if you say so," Mandie replied. She had not seen Sallie, or Sallie's grandfather, Uncle Ned, the old Cherokee friend of Mandie's father, since the Christmas holidays, and she was anxious to get caught up on all the news. She would also like to see her father's house down the road from the Woodards', where she had lived until her father died there. "Joe, do you think we could stop by my father's house?"

"Of course, Mandie," Joe replied. "You know Mr. Jacob Smith has moved in, like you asked him to, and he is taking care of the place. I'm sure he will be glad to see you."

"And I'll be glad to see him," Mandie replied as her thoughts turned back to the time when her father was living. She missed him so much.

Chapter 3 / A Pile of Mica

Even though dawn was just beginning to crack the night sky when Mandie got up the next morning and went downstairs, she found out from Mrs. Miller that her uncle John was already gone. And so was Dr. Woodard, who was making some early sick calls.

"Your uncle left about fifteen minutes ago, and Dr. Woodard just this minute drove off in his buggy," Mrs. Miller explained while she was cooking breakfast on the iron cookstove. "You just sit down over there at the table."

"Has Joe been down yet?" Mandie asked, pulling out a chair from the table and sitting down.

"Yes, he went down to the barn with his father. I suppose he'll be right back," Mrs. Miller explained. She stirred a pot of grits.

"I see Snowball already has his breakfast," Mandie said with a smile as she watched her white cat hurriedly eating from a bowl by the stove.

"Well, you know how it is. I couldn't make the poor little cat wait for scraps from the table," Mrs. Miller replied with a little laugh.

"Oh, that poor little cat will eat anything anytime you give it to him," Mandie replied, smiling at the woman.

Joe came in the back door as Mandie was speaking, and he added, "And so will this poor little boy. Mmmm! Something smells good." He walked over to the stove to look into the pots.

"Now you just go set yourself down there at the table and I'll bring the food," Mrs. Miller admonished him with a spoon in her hand. "Your mother is sleeping late."

"Yes, ma'am," Joe replied with a smile. He pulled out a chair across the table from Mandie and sat down. He looked back across the room at Mrs. Miller and teased, "I'm sitting down at the table now and I don't see any food."

"If I didn't know you better, and having changed your diapers when you were a baby, I'd say you're just plain uppity," Mrs. Miller answered with an effort to keep from laughing.

"And if I didn't know how good your cooking is, I'd say you're a pokey cook," Joe returned, grinning.

"There now. We're even. Nobody won," Mrs. Miller said, bringing a platter of bacon and eggs to the table and placing it in the middle. "'Course, now, if you don't want to eat my cooking, why, that's just fine with me. Just one less to cook for." She squeezed Joe's shoulder as she passed him. "Now let me get the rest of the food." She went back to the stove to ladle up grits into a bowl.

"If I didn't know better, I'd say you two don't like

each other," Mandie said, reaching for the platter. "But count me out. I'm hungry, and I want to eat so we can get going."

"And where are y'all off to today?" Mrs. Miller asked as she brought the bowl of hot grits to the table and set it in front of them.

"Here and there," Joe replied, helping himself to the grits. "We're going to see Sallie, and we're going by Mandie's father's house to see Mr. Jacob Smith. But we'll be back in time for supper. I thought maybe we could take a biscuit or two to tide us over." He smiled up at the dark-haired woman.

"A biscuit or two?" Mrs. Miller asked. She walked toward the cabinet and took down a small picnic basket. "I'll just pack this while y'all eat."

"Thank you, Mrs. Miller. I'm sure we will appreciate that when noontime comes," Mandie said, eating her bacon and eggs. Looking at Joe, she asked, "Do your mother and father know where we're going?"

"Oh yes, I told them last night, and I mentioned it again to my father this morning," Joe answered. He reached for a hot biscuit and buttered it.

"I wanted to be sure since Uncle John had told me not to go running off somewhere," Mandie said. "Soon as I finish eating, I'll get my shawl and be ready to go."

"And you'd better take a jacket, Joe," Mrs. Miller told him. She was quickly splitting open biscuits and inserting sausage patties in them as she wrapped them in a napkin. "I know it will be warming up later in the day, but it's downright chilly this morning."

"Yes, ma'am, I agree," Joe said, hurrying to eat everything on his plate. Looking across the room at

Mrs. Miller, he asked, "Could we please have some of that chocolate cake we had left from supper last night? It's not warm enough to melt it in the basket."

"Oh, Joe, you think of everything," Mandie said with a big smile.

"I'll put two large slices in the basket," Mrs. Miller replied, still piling up food to give them.

"We're going to have a picnic," Mandie said, happily watching the woman. "It's going to be a great day, a better day than I've had in a long time."

Joe looked at her and smiled. She felt herself blush and dropped her gaze. Hastily finishing her meal, she hurried to get her shawl. All the time she was thinking that it had been an awfully long time since she and Joe had had a picnic. And it would probably be a long time before they could get together again and have another one, especially if Joe had to stay in school all summer. Maybe she and her other friends could go down to New Orleans and visit Joe at his college if he didn't come home. But then that probably wouldn't work out too well. Joe would be too busy studying to spend any time with them. She and Joe had been friends all her life. How could she stand it if he didn't get home all summer and then wouldn't have any holidays until next Christmas? That would be positively, absolutely, unbearably awful! Something was going to have to be worked out. She'd figure out some solution to the problem.

Joe was waiting for her when Mandie came back to the kitchen.

"I was thinking, maybe you'd like to ride," Joe told her. "We have several horses now that would be tame enough for you."

Mandie thought for a second. "It would be nice to go horseback riding, but we couldn't go off the road whenever we took a notion," she replied. "If we cut through the woods down by the schoolhouse, it's too overgrown for a horse to get through. Besides, I have to take Snowball. I'm afraid he'll get out while I'm gone."

"All right," Joe agreed. "That's fine. I need the exercise anyway. I haven't had much time for walking." He picked up the picnic basket from the table.

Mrs. Miller was washing the dishes. "Y'all be careful, now, going through the woods. It's warm enough that snakes are beginning to crawl."

Mandie looked at Joe and said, "If you'd like to take your rifle along, I could carry the basket. And I can make Snowball walk on his leash part of the way." She stooped down to fasten the red collar and leash on Snowball.

"Good idea," Joe said. "I just cleaned my rifle yesterday. I'll get it." He went into the pantry and brought it out with some extra ammunition in a small drawstring bag, the kind that smoking tobacco came in. "Now we are prepared."

"Let's go," Mandie agreed, picking up the picnic basket. It was not very large and was not very heavy. She'd have no problem carrying it. Deciding to carry her white cat part of the way, she put him on her shoulder.

"Want to go by my father's house first and see Mr. Jacob Smith?" Mandie asked as they walked up the driveway to the road.

"If that's what you'd rather do, but I was thinking we'd find Sallie at the school if we go straight there, and then we could stop by to see Mr. Smith on our way home," Joe suggested. He looked at her for her answer.

"You're right," Mandie agreed. "It would be better to try and catch Sallie at the school. Otherwise, we'll have to go all the way to Uncle Ned's house to look for her."

Sallie Sweetwater was Uncle Ned's granddaughter, and she lived with him and her grandmother, Morning Star, at Deep Creek. Mandie was one-fourth Cherokee, and she had Cherokee relatives who lived at Bird-town, which was on the way to Deep Creek.

The morning air was cool, but as they walked they warmed up and removed their wraps. Mandie set Snowball down to walk and rolled up her shawl and stuck it through the handle of the basket she was carrying. Joe threw his jacket across his shoulder. They walked on down the dirt road, skipping over deep ruts here and there made by wagons and buggies in the winter during heavy rains. Snowball walked along with them, but now and then he tried to dart off the road in pursuit of some wild animal— a squirrel or bird—that went through the brush.

Neither one was talking much. Mandie looked up at Joe by her side and decided he must have grown six inches since she last saw him. "You are outgrowing me," she said with a smile. "But just wait, I'll catch up one day soon."

Joe laughed out loud and teased, "Catch up? I hope not. Girls shouldn't get so tall, and I don't think you will add more than a couple of inches by the time you are grown, if that much."

Mandie straightened up and stretched as she replied, "I hope I get a lot taller so I can look you in the eye." She grinned at him.

"That will never be," Joe answered, also straightening up and looking down at her.

"Well, I won't be fourteen until June, and people sometimes grow until they are about eighteen years old, so I have four years to do it," Mandie reminded him.

They were near the crossing on the Little Tennessee River as they followed the Tomahawk Trail, and at that moment Snowball managed to get loose from his leash and ran off down the mountainside.

"Oh, the hook came undone!" Mandie exclaimed as she started after the cat with the leash in her hand.

"Leave the basket here," Joe quickly called out as he laid down his rifle and reached for the basket, which Mandie gave him as she ran on.

Leaving the basket by his rifle, he followed Mandie and she suddenly stopped in front of him.

"Joe! Look!" Mandie exclaimed, pointing across the mountainous terrain.

Joe stopped to look in the direction she was pointing.

"Look at that pile of mica!" Mandie told him. Snowball was already down in the gap sniffing around the mica mound.

"Now, how did that mica get there?" Joe asked in disbelief. "There's no mica mine in this area that I know of."

The two stood and surveyed the mound. Then Mandie realized she had better go after Snowball before he got farther away. She started down the mountainside. "Snowball, come back here!" she yelled as she carefully stepped down the rocks.

Joe was right behind her. "Do be careful, Mandie," he said. "I don't want you falling down and getting hurt, and then I would have to carry you home."

Mandie didn't dare look back to see if Joe was teasing. She slowly made her way down the slope toward the cat. And she was glad to see Snowball had not run off any farther away. He seemed to be fascinated with the mica and was walking around smelling it. Vivid sparkles twinkled all over the shiny mica as the sun's rays touched it, making it look like a thousand lights on the mound. It was blinding in the sunshine.

"Snowball!" Mandie called to him when she finally reached the level ground. "You come here immediately!" She hurried toward him.

For once, Snowball didn't play games and run away from her as he usually did when he got off the leash. He stood there looking at his mistress and gave one loud meow when she stooped to fasten the leash back to his collar.

"Did the hook on the leash break?" Joe asked, coming up behind her.

"No, it seems to be all right. I suppose I just didn't fasten it right," Mandie replied, standing up and holding firmly to the red leash.

"Thank goodness that cat didn't decide to run on over the mountain somewhere," Joe said with a big sigh. He walked around and looked at the mica mound. "I just don't understand how all this got down here."

"And where did it come from?" Mandie asked as she also surveyed the shining mound. "Why would anyone dump all this down here?"

"Dump all this down here?" Joe said, smiling down at her. "I would imagine it took quite a long time to dump all this down here and a lot of work. Some foolhardy notion."

"Maybe Sallie knows something about it," Mandie suggested, looking up at Joe. "The Cherokee people usually know about everything that goes on anywhere near them."

"Let's get going," Joe said. "We can ask Sallie about it."

"Come on, Snowball," Mandie said to the cat as she pulled on the leash and started up the slope.

"Let me hold on to that cat going back up, and you hold my hand," Joe told her, reaching for the leash. "I'm afraid you might slide down."

Mandie smiled up at him as she handed over the leash and he reached to grasp her hand. "Just be sure you don't slide and take us all down with you," she cautioned him. She felt the warmth of his hand and immediately became shy with her old friend. Here was that strange feeling again. *What is wrong?* she wondered.

As soon as they were safely to the top of the slope, Mandie quickly removed her hand and went to pick up the picnic basket with her shawl still through the handle. Joe had thrown down his jacket with his rifle, and he picked them up, still holding the end of Snowball's leash.

"I'll either hold on to Snowball the rest of the way, or I can carry the basket," Joe offered.

"But you have your rifle to carry," Mandie replied, holding on to the basket.

"I know," Joe replied. "Here, I'll take the basket and you can carry this cat so he won't be able to get away again." He handed her the end of the leash and reached for the basket. "We also have to cross the river, you know."

Mandie handed him the basket and put Snowball on her shoulder. "I can manage Snowball all right," she assured him as they walked on, but she was secretly worrying about getting across the river on the swinging bridge while balancing with Snowball in her arms. She had been on that bridge before and she knew how it would start swinging the minute someone stepped on it.

She felt Joe had read her mind when he said, "Now, when we get to the river, I'll run across with Snowball and tie him to a bush or something, and then I'll come back and get you across. I know that cat doesn't like that bridge any more than you do." He looked down at Mandie and smiled.

"Thanks" was all Mandie could think of to say. After they crossed the Little Tennessee River, they would also have to cross the Tuckasegee River, but that was not a big problem. The crossing was shallow and covered with rocks to step on. The Cherokee school and also the Cherokee hospital were both not very far from the other side of the Tuckasegee River.

After what seemed like ages to Mandie, they finally got across both rivers without any incidents and the Cherokee schoolhouse soon came in sight.

"At last!" she exclaimed as they walked toward it. She held Snowball on his leash and had draped her shawl over her arm.

"Have you been here since the schoolhouse was finished?" Joe asked. He was carrying the basket and his rifle with his jacket thrown over his shoulder.

"The building was finished, but the desks that had been ordered had not arrived when I was here the last time," Mandie replied.

"I understand from my father that it's all complete now," Joe told her. "And the Cherokee people are beginning to use their hospital now and then. He has had a patient or two in there, and some of the Indians living near here have been working there, taking care of everything."

"I'm so glad the Cherokee people have finally decided to use it," Mandie replied with a smile. "I was afraid they would never get over their suspicion about the gold that built it. They said it had a curse on it, remember?"

"Yes, but it was great that we found all that gold in the cave and used it for the hospital," Joe replied. "If you want to, we could go on to the hospital after we see Sallie at the school. She would know if anyone is at the hospital right now."

"Oh yes, let's do," Mandie agreed, looking ahead at the building in the distance.

The schoolhouse was constructed of hand-hewn logs, with a huge rock chimney rising in the center of the roof. The building stood two feet off the ground on rock pillars with space for storage beneath. A large iron bell hung at the end of the full-length front porch. The front door was in the center with glass windows on either side, protected by wooden shutters.

Mandie looked up at Joe and said, "I like it better than our old schoolhouse at Charley Gap."

"Of course," Joe agreed. "This is all new and ours was a real antique. This one is larger than ours, too."

They stepped up on the porch and Joe opened the door, allowing Mandie to step inside first. Mandie picked up Snowball and entered the schoolhouse. Sallie was sitting at the head of the room and there were four small pupils at desks in front of her.

The Indian girl rose and smiled as she saw them.

"Mandie! Joe!" Sallie exclaimed, coming to meet them. "I'm so glad to see you both."

The girls quickly embraced and then stepped back to look at each other, while Joe stood by.

"Sallie, it seems so long since I saw you, but it was really just at the Christmas holidays," Mandie said with a big smile for her friend.

Sallie Sweetwater was almost a year older than Mandie, and she had long black hair held back by a red ribbon. She wore mocassins and a long, full skirt with a ruffled blouse and a strand of multi-colored beads. Her black eyes sparkled with joy at seeing her friends.

"That is too long," Sallie said. Looking up at Joe to include him, she added, "I wish both of you could live nearer, but I know that is not possible until we all get educated. I hope you like your college, Joe."

"It's a lot of hard work, but I do enjoy it," Joe told her.

"Maybe you and I can go to his college," Mandie told Sallie.

The pupils had turned to look and began talking among themselves.

"Oh maybe," Sallie said, turning back to the children. "Read. I said read now. Do not talk." She watched them until they obeyed her.

"You sure have them trained well," Joe said with a laugh.

"Yes, the little ones are obedient. It is the older ones who give trouble," Sallie explained. "Here we stand, talking. Come on in and sit down. I see you brought Snowball." She walked over to a back corner of the room and motioned for them to sit on a bench with her there.

"Does Mr. O'Neal still live in the room at the back?" Mandie asked, sitting down and holding tightly to Snowball's leash as he curled up at her feet.

Joe laid down his rifle, set the basket on the bench, and joined the girls.

"Yes, Mr. O'Neal lives back there, but he is not here right now," Sallie said. "He had to go into town to post some mail."

"Are you actually teaching these children?" Joe asked.

Sallie laughed and said, "Only now and then, when Mr. O'Neal has to be out. He has certain days of the week for the different ages, and today it's the little ones, five- and six-year-olds."

"But aren't you going to school yourself?" Mandie asked.

"Yes, I am, but on certain days with other pupils my age," Sallie explained. "This is much better and much nearer than going away over the mountain to the other school I attended, and Mr. O'Neal is a good teacher. I am learning more here."

"Is Tsa'ni still going around fussing because the white people came down here from Boston to build a school for the Cherokee children?" Mandie asked.

Tsa'ni was the grandson of Mandie's father's uncle, and he did not like white people. His grandfather was the brother of Mandie's grandmother, a beautiful Cherokee girl who had married Mandie's white grandfather, both of whom had died many years ago.

"He is always saying bad things about white people, and instead of coming here, he still goes all the way over the mountain to that school I used to attend," Sallie explained. "The other school was built by the Cherokee people a long time ago and has a Cherokee teacher and nothing but Cherokee pupils, which is what Tsa'ni likes. He will never learn very much if he does not get out into the world of the white people."

Mandie suddenly remembered the mound of mica. "Sallie, we saw this huge pile of mica on our way here, on the other side of the Little Tennessee River," she said. "Do you know anything about it?"

Sallie looked at her and asked with a frown, "A pile of mica? No, I have not seen a pile of mica anywhere near here."

"It was down in the gap by the trail before we got to the Little Tennessee River coming this way," Joe explained. "It certainly didn't belong down there. There is no mica anywhere around here that I know of. But we couldn't figure out how it got there."

Sallie shook her head and said, "That is very strange. No one lives near the place you are talking about, do they?"

"No, I don't remember seeing any houses near there, but of course there could have been some back in the woods along the way," Joe replied.

"Sallie, if we wait for you to finish here today, could you go with us and see this mica mound?" Mandie asked.

"No, I am sorry, but I promised Mr. O'Neal I would remain here until he returns late this afternoon. The children will also be here until then," Sallie replied. "Maybe you all could come back tomorrow and we could go look at it then."

"All right," Mandie agreed, looking at Joe. "That is, if you want to."

"Sure," Joe agreed. "But tomorrow is Tuesday, and your uncle will be back for you anytime from

Wednesday on, remember. So if you plan to visit any of your Cherokee kinpeople at Bird-town, or Uncle Ned and Morning Star, then we'll have to work out some time schedule to get that all in."

Mandie sighed and said, "I suppose I'll have to let my kinpeople wait until later. I can come back this summer. And speaking of summer, Sallie, we wanted to ask you about all of us and Jonathan and Celia getting together this summer, remember?"

"I have not forgotten and my grandfather has agreed," Sallie said with a smile. "I will tell him to-night that you are at Joe's house and will be back tomorrow. He will help us make our plans."

"That's fine," Joe agreed. Then, glancing at the picnic basket, he said, "Sallie, would you like to eat with us? Mrs. Miller packed this basket full of food, and I'm getting a little hungry."

"Thank you for asking me," Sallie told him. "Then I will be able to give the children the food I had brought. These little ones do not have much to eat sometimes."

Sallie spread out her food at the front desk for the children and then returned to her friends where they ate on the bench. They made plans that Mandie and Joe would return the next day and Sallie would go with them to see the mica mound.

Chapter 4 / Lots of Thinking

When they left the Cherokee schoolhouse, Mandie decided it was too late in the day to go see the Cherokee hospital.

"I'd rather go on back and stop by to see Mr. Jacob Smith instead of going on to the Cherokee hospital today," Mandie told Joe as they walked up the lane from the schoolhouse to the main road. "Maybe we could go over there tomorrow when we come back."

"All right, fine," Joe agreed. He had put on his jacket and was carrying the empty basket and his rifle. "I don't think it's all that warm today."

"I agree," Mandie said, winding her shawl around her shoulders while she held on to Snowball's leash.

"If you want to go straight to see Mr. Smith, we could cut through the woods, which would be faster than going down the trail," Joe told her as they walked on.

"Good idea," Mandie said. "That way I'll have a few minutes longer to visit with Mr. Smith."

They still had to cross back over both the rivers, but when they got to the other side, Joe led the way through a dense forest. Mandie had to pick Snowball up and carry him. There was barely enough room to walk between the bushes here and there, and she didn't want him to get away again. Therefore, they didn't go back by the mica mound.

Mandie had never been on the route Joe was taking her. Nothing was familiar to her. She called to him as he walked ahead, pushing back bushes, "Are you sure you know where you are going?"

Joe stopped to look back at her, grinned, and said, "I know every crack and corner of this countryside around here. Are you worried that we might be lost?"

Mandie smiled at him and replied, "No, not lost, just going around in circles maybe. Do you really think this is a shortcut?"

Joe was standing still, looking at her, as he said, "Sure it's a shortcut. I've been through here many times. Remember, I grew up in this countryside. We're going to come out not far behind your father's property."

"If you say so," Mandie agreed as Joe started on and she followed, holding tightly to Snowball. She hoped he was right.

The two walked on awhile longer. Conversation was impossible with Joe going ahead, making a trail, and Mandie dodging limbs to keep from getting scratched and keeping Snowball grasped in her arms as he tried to get down. She was sorry she had not insisted on going back the way they had come. It might be longer but at least it was easy walking.

Just as a briar caught Mandie's coat, causing her to pause to break it loose, Joe suddenly stopped and yelled back, "Stop! Wait!" He didn't look back at her and grabbed his rifle off his shoulder.

Mandie held her breath as she froze in her tracks and watched. "What is it?" she asked in a loud whisper. She held tightly to her white cat.

Joe didn't answer but quickly fired his rifle at the bushes ahead of him. Then he slowly moved forward, keeping his eyes on the distant underbrush. Snowball growled and stuck his claws in the shoulder of Mandie's coat.

Mandie felt her heart start pounding. Some danger lurked ahead. She held her breath and didn't move as she watched Joe.

Then Joe suddenly turned around with a big grin on his face. "I got him!" he yelled back to her.

Mandie finally stepped forward. "What was it?" she asked.

Joe hurried back to her and said, "Just what Mrs. Miller told us to watch out for. A snake!" he touched her arm to turn her around. "Now let's cut through over here. This way," he said, leading her away from the place where he had shot the snake.

Mandie started trembling in spite of herself and said in a shaky voice, "A snake! Oh, Joe, I'm so glad you brought your rifle. Don't you think we ought to get out of these woods?"

"That's exactly what we're doing," Joe explained, still holding her arm. "There's an opening through here where we can reach the road."

In a moment Mandie saw the break in the bushes and the main road beyond. She felt so relieved, but she couldn't stop herself from shaking a little. She allowed Joe to guide her out onto the road, and once there she stopped and took a deep breath and said, trying to smile, "End of our journey through the woods, right?"

"Yes, I'm sorry, Mandie," Joe said, suddenly moving his hand from her arm to put it around her shoulders and squeeze hard.

Mandie felt her face flush and she tried to smile as she said, "It wasn't your fault. Neither one of us knew it would be there, but thanks to Mrs. Miller's warning you were prepared." She quickly moved away from his arm and added, "Now let's get on our way to see Mr. Jacob Smith."

Joe instantly fell into step with her and they hurried down the road. The sun was already dropping near the top of the mountain. Pretty soon it would begin to get shadowy with the sunshine gone, even though it was not that late in the day. Not long after that the darkness of the night would envelop the place.

When they finally reached the intersection of the road to her father's house, Mandie quickened her steps and kept her gaze ahead, watching for the log cabin to come into sight. And when she finally saw the chimney through the trees, she caught her breath and hurried still faster until she came to the lane where the old house stood.

"Oh, Joe, Mr. Smith has fixed things up," she declared as she looked around, going down the lane. Everything looked nice and neat and well kept—the yard, the old barn, and the house itself.

"Yes, he has," Joe agreed, following her to the front porch.

Mandie felt tears come into her blue eyes as she stepped up to knock on the front door. She had so many happy memories of living here with her father until his death. In her mind she could see him stopping his work on the rail fence to wave to her when she came home from school every day. And she noticed that Mr. Smith had finished the fence as she glanced across the yard. Finally she raised her hand and knocked. There was no answer.

"I'm afraid he must be gone," Joe told her as she knocked again.

Mandie knocked a third time. Finally she turned back to Joe. "Maybe he's in the barn," she said, going down the steps.

"I doubt it. He would have heard us," Joe told her as he followed.

They stepped inside the barn and looked around. He was not there.

"You see, his horse is gone," Joe said.

"Maybe his horse is out in the pasture," Mandie said hopefully.

"I don't believe so. His saddle is also gone," Joe replied, pointing up to the rack where it was kept.

"Does he not have a cow or chickens, or anything?" Mandie asked as she looked around and went back outside.

Joe followed her and replied, "No, not yet, just his horse. He buys milk and eggs from neighbors. He said he wanted to be free to travel back and forth to his old house in the mountains until he gets completely moved and settled in here. Then he will begin farming."

"Do you think he may be gone to his old house now?" Mandie asked.

"I'm sorry, but I have no idea as to where he has gone, Mandie," Joe said, looking around the fields. "I saw him Friday when I came home from college. In fact, I told him we were expecting you at our house sometime during the spring holidays, and he said he looked forward to seeing you again."

"Do you think we could come back tomorrow and maybe find him at home?" Mandie asked, turning to look all around the yard, still holding on to Snowball.

"Of course we will come back tomorrow and see if he has returned," Joe promised.

Mandie didn't reply but started up the lane and quickly turned off onto the road that led up the mountain to the cemetery where her father was buried. Joe silently followed.

When she reached the top, Mandie ran to her father's grave and knelt down. Snowball managed to escape unnoticed. Through a sudden rush of tears she noticed there were spring wildflowers on it. With a terrible pain in her heart, she murmured, "Oh, God, please take care of my daddy!"

Joe had come to her side, and he put an arm around her shoulders.

"He will, Mandie. He will," he whispered in her ear as he drew her closer to him.

Mandie sat on the ground, still sobbing, and allowed Joe to pull her over against his shoulder. She remembered the day so vividly almost two years before when her father had been laid in his grave. And it hurt as bad now as it had then to look at the mound of earth. *Why, oh why, did he have to die?*

The two sat there a long time, Joe silent and Mandie's sobs finally ending. She straightened up and wiped her tear-stained face with the end of her shawl. "I'm sorry, Joe," she said, trying to catch her breath.

Joe reached with his handkerchief to dry her tears. "Sorry for what, Mandie?" he asked. "I understand, but I certainly wouldn't understand if you didn't shed any tears. I know how much you loved your father."

Mandie allowed him to dab at her eyes with his handkerchief.

Suddenly she heard a loud, angry meowing and quickly looked around. "Snowball!" she said, standing up.

Joe jumped up and looked over at the road. "I see him," he said. "He didn't get very far. His leash is tangled up in the bushes." He went over to pick up the cat and had to unhook his leash to get him free.

"I'll hold him," Mandie said as she came up behind Joe.

Joe handed the white cat to Mandie and bent down to untangle the leash. "I suppose it would be safer if we put this back on, don't you think?"

"Yes, we'd better," Mandie agreed as Joe found the ring on the cat's collar and snapped the leash back in place.

Mandie started down the road, and Joe picked up his rifle and the basket and silently followed. Neither said a word until they reached the driveway to the Woodards' house. Then they both stopped.

"Could we go by first thing in the morning to see if Mr. Smith has come back before we go to meet Sallie?" Mandie asked.

Joe smiled and said, "That is what I was going to suggest. Then if he is not back we can come by there again on our way home tomorrow afternoon."

"Thanks, Joe," Mandie said, quickly squeezing Joe's hand that was holding the basket.

They hurried down the driveway to the Woodards' house and were both surprised to find Uncle

Ned, Mandie's father's old Cherokee friend, sitting in the parlor with Dr. Woodard.

"Uncle Ned, I'm so glad you came," Mandie said, putting Snowball down and unhooking his leash. She removed her shawl and threw it on a chair as she hurried to the old man sitting by the fireplace. Snowball went to curl up on the hearth.

"Nice to see you, Uncle Ned," Joe added, stepping forward to the warmth of the fire after he left his rifle and the basket in the hallway.

"John Shaw send message," Uncle Ned told Mandie as she sat down near him and Dr. Woodard.

"Uncle John sent a message?" Mandie asked. "But where did you see Uncle John?"

"Not see," Uncle Ned explained. "John Shaw see Jessan, son of Wirt, in Asheville. Jessan take baskets to sell in Asheville. John Shaw see him. Tell Jessan when he come home today to tell Dr. Woodard he not be back till Saturday. He busy with business."

Mandie's blue eyes grew wide with happiness. "Saturday! Then I get to stay that much longer!" she exclaimed, looking at Joe.

Joe smiled at her and said, "I was hoping for a miracle."

"Thank you, Uncle Ned, for coming to let me know," Mandie told him.

"Sallie say you come back to school tomorrow," Uncle Ned said. "See mica."

"Oh yes," Mandie replied, and she explained to him and Dr. Woodard about finding the mound of mica.

"I don't remember ever seeing any mica in that particular place," Dr. Woodard said.

"No place for mica," Uncle Ned agreed. "Wrong place. We see."

"Are you going with us tomorrow, Uncle Ned?" Joe asked.

The old man nodded and said, "Dr. Woodard say I stay here tonight. So I go with you when sun come up."

Mandie looked at Dr. Woodard and asked, "Dr. Woodard, do you have any idea where Mr. Jacob Smith is? We came by there and he wasn't home."

"And his horse was gone," Joe added.

"No, I haven't seen him since last week, but I wouldn't imagine he has gone far because he knew you were coming any day," the doctor replied.

Mandie looked back at Uncle Ned and explained, "We thought we would go by to see Mr. Smith first thing in the morning on our way to see Sallie."

"Fine, we go see," Uncle Ned agreed.

At that moment Mrs. Woodard came into the parlor. She looked around the room and said, "Now that we're all here, I believe it's time to go and eat supper. Mrs. Miller has been keeping it warm for us."

"I need to clean up," Joe said, rising from the chair where he was sitting next to Mandie. "It'll only take me a couple of minutes, Mother." He started to leave the room, glanced back at Mandie, and said, "Your face is dirty, Mandie." He grinned at her.

Mandie quickly stood up and said, "I know it's bound to be after all we've been through today. I'll run up to my room and wash."

"Both of you, now don't be too long," Mrs. Woodard cautioned them as she sat down in the chair vacated by Mandie.

"Yes, ma'am, I'll hurry," Mandie called back to her. She followed Joe out the door into the hallway.

"That was not very nice of you, telling me my face was dirty in front of everybody," Mandie said with a slight frown as they went down the hallway.

Joe stopped and turned back to look at her. "I just wanted to tell you something without everyone hearing." He smiled at her.

"Tell me something? Like what?" Mandie asked, standing in front of him.

Joe looked at her and then shifted his gaze over her head as he said, "Like—like—" he looked directly into her blue eyes and finished—"like, oh shucks, Mandie, I've missed you something awful, just knowing I was so far away in New Orleans and you were in school in Asheville." He quickly cleared his throat and added, "That's what I wanted to say. That's all."

Mandie felt herself cloaked in happiness. Joe really missed her. "I've missed you, too, Joe," she told him. "Even though it hasn't been a real long time since I saw you, it has felt like years." Then she quickly added, "Now we'd better get washed up or your mother will come looking for us." Mandie started to walk on down the hallway.

Joe followed Mandie and said, "I'll work real hard and try to get enough time off from school to come home at least for a few days this summer."

Mandie felt giggly silly as she told him, "You'd better or I might just find some other boy who likes to solve mysteries." She kept walking.

Joe reached forward and grasped her hand to stop her and turn her around to face him. "You'd better not do that because I might not like it," he said, looking down at her.

"But you must have pretty girls down at the college," Mandie teased, her blue eyes sparkling with laughter.

"There are some girls there. I told you that, but I wouldn't know whether they're pretty or not. I haven't talked to any of them," Joe replied. "And I don't want to talk to any of them. I'll save all my talk for you when I come back."

"Joe, let me go," Mandie said with a laugh as she pulled her hand free. "I don't want your mother holding up supper because of us." She turned to go up the stairs. "I'll get washed and beat you back to the parlor." She ran up the steps two at a time.

Joe followed and turned down the opposite end of the hallway upstairs. "You'd better hurry, then," he called to her.

Mandie rushed on down to the room she used when she visited the Woodards. "What a silly conversation," she mumbled to herself. "What has got into Joe, and me, too, I suppose?" She hummed to herself as she thought about it.

She quickly went to the washstand in her room, poured water from the pitcher into the bowl, and washed her face and hands. Then she went over to the bureau, unbraided her blond hair, and brushed it out. Quickly finding a ribbon in the drawer she tied it back. "That ought to look better," she said to herself as she looked in the mirror.

She rushed to open the door to the hallway and hesitated. "Joe is really growing up, but I don't think I am," she said aloud to herself as she paused with her hand on the doorknob. Then she added, "Or maybe I am and I don't know it." She giggled to herself and went out into the hall. She wasn't sure she wanted to grow up yet, but what could she do about it? Nothing, absolutely nothing.

Deep in thought she went on down the stairs to join the others in the parlor.

Chapter 5 / Here We Go Again!

The next morning everyone got up early and ate breakfast together. They made their plans for the day.

"How did you get here, Uncle Ned?" Joe asked the old man. "Did you drive your wagon?"

"No, ride horse," Uncle Ned replied, finishing his cup of coffee.

Mrs. Woodard spoke up, "Then, Joe, you should hitch up my cart for you and Amanda."

Dr. Woodard pushed back from the table and stood up. "Yes, do that, Joe," he said. "Now I must get going. I have to go all the way over the mountain to see about Mrs. Coleman." He walked up behind his wife's chair and bent to plant a kiss on her cheek with a whispered, "Love you."

Mrs. Woodard squeezed his hand and said, "Be careful, darling."

"Uncle Ned, nice to have seen you. Come back soon," Dr. Woodard said as he got his coat and hat

from the pegs by the back door and put them on.
He took down his medical bag from the shelf above.

"Soon," Uncle Ned agreed as he, too, rose from
the table. "Must come see my house soon, too."

"We will," Dr. Woodard promised as he opened
the back door. "You young ones don't get into any
trouble today."

"We won't," Mandie and Joe said together as
the doctor went out the back door.

"I think I'll wear my cloak today," Mandie said,
pushing her chair away from the table. "I'll get it
and be right back down."

Joe got up and went to get his coat from the
pegs. "All right," he said. "I'll see about the cart.
Meet you at the barn."

Mandie rushed upstairs and got her cloak. By
the time she got back downstairs the kitchen was
empty, except for Snowball. He came to meet her
with a loud meow from where he had been eating
near the cookstove.

"Yes, I know you want to go, too. You always
do," Mandie said, stooping to fasten his red leash to
his collar and then picking him up. "Let's go."

When she got to the barn, Uncle Ned had sad-
dled his horse and Joe had the cart waiting.

"Don't forget. We're going by to see Mr. Jacob
Smith first, aren't we?" Mandie reminded them.

"Of course," Joe agreed.

"Yes," Uncle Ned said.

Mandie jumped into the cart and they started
down the road to Mr. Smith's. Uncle Ned followed.
When they got there, Mandie was disappointed
again. There was no sign of Mr. Smith. Joe promised they would come by again on their way home
that afternoon.

Since they were riding and it wouldn't take long to get to the place where they had seen the mica mound, they decided to go there next.

"It's down the slope over there," Joe called to Uncle Ned as he halted the cart and he and Mandie jumped down. She carried Snowball.

Uncle Ned dismounted and tethered his horse to a bush nearby.

Mandie walked over to look down the slope and quickly turned to Joe. "Are you sure this is where we saw the mica?" she asked.

"Yes," Joe replied as he and Uncle Ned came to stand by Mandie. "Oh no!" he added.

"It's gone!" Mandie exclaimed.

Uncle Ned looked around the area and asked, "Sure this place?"

"Yes, it is the right place," Joe replied. Turning to Mandie, he said, "Remember Snowball ran down there and we went down to get him? Remember the way we went down those rocks there?" He pointed down the slope.

"Yes, I recognize some of the rocks and bushes," Mandie replied. "But how did that whole mound of mica disappear? And where did it go?"

"That's what I'd like to know, too," Joe said, frowning as he paced back and forth.

"The mica was down there in that big clearing," Mandie explained, pointing below.

Uncle Ned looked in that direction and said, "Go, look, see." He started down the slope.

Joe asked Mandie, "Why don't you tie Snowball in the cart if you're going down there, too?"

"It would be easier without him," Mandie agreed and walked back to the cart.

Joe came to help her fasten Snowball's leash to

a rope tied on a hook inside the cart. "There, now, he'll be safe," he said.

The two hurried back to follow Uncle Ned, who was already going down the hill. Mandie tried to catch up with him.

"Don't rush so or you may slide down," Joe warned Mandie as they stepped down the rocks on the hillside. "No hurry now. That mica's long gone."

"I know, but we might find it some other place down there," Mandie told him. She didn't dare look up at him for fear of making a wrong step and falling. "It has to be somewhere. It couldn't have just— gone away—evaporated."

"Well, it's sure not here now," Joe said.

They got down to the plateau and saw Uncle Ned bending over now and then to look at the ground. Mandie knew he was probably trying to trace tracks of some kind.

"The mound was over there next to that line of trees," Mandie told him, pointing to the left.

"Yes, see," the old man told her, walking to the place she indicated. He bent to scoop a handful of loose dirt and held it out to them. "Mica. See."

Mandie and Joe both looked at the dirt as he scattered it back on the ground. Particles of mica sparkled like diamonds as it fell.

"I don't understand how a mound of mica that big could just disappear overnight," Mandie said.

"Was big?" Uncle Ned asked.

"Oh yes, sir," Joe told him. "It was higher than a house and at least thirty feet long."

"We find trail," Uncle Ned told them. He led the way along the trees, stooping now and then to check the ground for mica particles. Mandie and

Joe helped. They were making progress until the clues went straight into the river. The three of them stood there gazing into the water.

"Do you suppose they dumped it all into the river?" Mandie asked.

"I don't think so," Joe said. "It would make the river overflow its banks, that much mica would."

"Yes, too much mica to be in river. Maybe part in river," Uncle Ned told them.

"But how can we find that out?" Mandie asked.

"We search river," the old man replied. "Look in water, see if mica in water."

"But I can't swim," Mandie protested.

"But I can," Joe said with a big grin.

"You'll get your clothes all wet if you go in the river," Mandie told him as she stood there staring at the water.

"We go get Sallie, and we go home for clothes," Uncle Ned explained.

"Oh yes, Sallie must be thinking we're never going to get there today," Mandie agreed. "Are you going to your house, Uncle Ned, to get a change of clothes?"

"Yes, my house," he agreed. "Then we come back, look in river."

"Do you think you might have some clothes I could borrow?" Joe asked. "Or should I go back to my house and get something to change into?"

"Plenty clothes at my house. Now we go," Uncle Ned said, turning back the way they had come.

Mandie hurried along with Joe and Uncle Ned, but she didn't much like the idea of them going into the river when she couldn't join them because she didn't know how to swim. One of these days she was going to learn to swim and surprise them all.

Almost everybody she knew could swim, even Sallie, and she hated being the only one who couldn't. She wondered why the fancy school she attended in Asheville, the Misses Heathwood's School for Girls, didn't teach swimming, but then she supposed it was not a ladylike thing to do. Sometimes her grandmother, Mrs. Taft, for all her wealth, acted in unladylike ways when it was not to her liking to do something. Maybe Mandie could talk her into allowing swimming lessons, wherever they taught such stuff. She would see about that.

"I think I hear that white cat," Joe called back to her as he hurried up the slope.

Mandie distinctly heard Snowball's angry meows. "He probably thinks we've forgotten about him," Mandie said, following Joe.

Uncle Ned, bringing up the rear, laughed and said, "White cat spoiled."

"I know he is," Mandie agreed as she stepped onto the road above. "But remember, Uncle Ned, Snowball is special. I brought him with me from my father's house when my father . . . when my father went to heaven." She looked up at the old man with tears in her eyes.

Uncle Ned embraced her and said, "Yes, white cat special."

Joe had already reached the cart and he called back, "No wonder he is yelling. His leash is all tangled up." He reached into the vehicle trying to get Snowball loose.

Mandie rushed to untangle her cat and then held him tightly in her arms. "I'm sorry, Snowball," she said, rubbing her face on his soft white fur. "I won't leave you alone again. I promise."

"Come on, Mandie. We've got to go," Joe called from his seat on the cart.

Mandie quickly glanced at Uncle Ned who was already on his horse. She rushed to step up into the cart.

As they rode along to the Cherokee school to pick up Sallie, Mandie thought again about asking Joe what it was that he was trying to tell her from the train when he had gone off to college. But she decided it was not the right time. She didn't want to try to discuss it while riding in the cart over the bumpy dirt road, jolting and swaying and having to hold on to her seat in some places. But she did need to make a certain time when it would be right to ask him about this.

When they arrived at the Cherokee school, Sallie was waiting just inside the schoolroom. Carrying Snowball on her shoulder, Mandie opened the door and saw the missionary schoolteacher, Riley O'Neal, sitting at the front of the room before quite a few Cherokee teenagers. Sallie rose from the bench by the door to greet her.

"Mandie, I am so glad you could come," Sallie said, and added as Joe came inside behind Mandie, "And you, too, Joe." She looked behind Joe and saw her grandfather. "And my grandfather is here, too." She was surprised.

With Mandie and Joe adding their comments, Uncle Ned quickly whispered to Sallie an explanation of what they were planning to do. They didn't want to disturb the class.

Then Mandie heard the schoolmaster rise and say to the pupils, "Keep reading your books. I will return in a few minutes to ask you questions." Riley O'Neal came quickly to the back to greet them.

"It is so nice to see everyone," he said, looking at Joe and Uncle Ned and then at Mandie. "And, Miss Amanda, it is always a pleasure to have you visit." He still had his Boston accent, Mandie noticed as she looked up at his smiling blue eyes.

"Thank you, Mr. O'Neal. I'm always happy to visit my friends," Mandie replied, thinking the Misses Heathwood would be pleased with her ladylike deportment.

Sallie began explaining to Riley O'Neal about the mica and its disappearance. Mandie noticed he seemed to be listening, but he continued to stare at her instead of Sallie, which made her feel uncomfortable. She moved closer to Uncle Ned to break Mr. O'Neal's line of vision but without any luck. Her face burned as she remembered how she had met the man. She had been running away from home and had slipped on the mountainside and came tumbling down right in front of his wagon. *Very embarrassing*, she thought. And now he was here to stay for a while at least. He had been able to get his missionary group to build this school to educate the Cherokee children.

"I regret that I cannot join you," Riley O'Neal was saying to Uncle Ned. "But as you see, I have students who will be here until two o'clock. That is if they don't get bored and decide to go home. Sallie here is very good at keeping them interested in their studies, even when it's impossible for me to do so on occasion. I am hoping she will become a teacher someday. She would make a very fine one." He looked at Sallie, then turned his gaze back on Mandie and said, "Is there any hope of making a teacher out of you?"

Mandie smiled at him and said, "I'm not sure

right now. All I can think of for the future would be to become a farmer like my father was."

Uncle Ned, Joe, and Sallie all smiled at this remark, but Mr. O'Neal frowned and said, "Well, now, we do have to have farmers or we would all starve to death."

Mandie felt as though he was teasing her with that remark. She turned to Uncle Ned and said, "If we are going all the way to your house and then back to the river, shouldn't we hurry? Mrs. Woodard is expecting Joe and me back before suppertime."

"Yes," Uncle Ned agreed.

They said their good-byes and started for the door. Riley O'Neal followed them and said, "Perhaps when I get finished here I can find you at the river, Uncle Ned."

"Yes, look there," the old man replied.

Snowball squirmed to get down, and Mandie hurried on outside to the cart. Sallie followed and asked, "Will you be going into the river also, Mandie?"

Mandie sighed and said, "No, Sallie. Remember, I don't know how to swim."

"I forgot," Sallie replied as they climbed up into the cart and Joe rushed after them.

Mandie looked back and saw Riley O'Neal hurrying to say something to Uncle Ned, who was mounting his horse. The old man nodded and rode over to the cart. Riley O'Neal went back to the schoolhouse front porch and stood there waving good-bye.

"He say wagons missing," Uncle Ned told Joe. "Do not leave cart alone."

"Wagons missing?" Mandie repeated, holding tightly to Snowball.

"Yes," Sallie said. "Dimar came by the school-house to tell us this morning that three wagons are missing. His mother's disappeared from their barn yesterday. Last night Jessan, father of Tsa'ni, could not find his wagon in their yard. Also, your uncle Wirt, father of Jessan, lost his wagon while it was in his barn."

Uncle Ned had been listening from where he sat on his horse and now he said, "We go my house."

The three young people discussed the missing wagons as they rode behind Uncle Ned to his house.

"As big as a wagon is, I don't see how anybody could steal a wagon and hide it," Joe remarked.

"But Dimar says he and Jessan have been searching all over the mountain and have not found one yet," Sallie said.

When they arrived at Uncle Ned's house, Morning Star, his wife, was not home. Uncle Ned said she had gone to visit sick people in the Cherokee hospital.

"I wish I had time to go to the hospital and see everything," Mandie remarked to Sallie as they waited in the cart for Uncle Ned and Joe to find clothes in the house that they could wear in the river.

"Perhaps the next time you visit you will have more time to see it," Sallie said.

"Don't forget we need to discuss with your grandfather our plans to visit each other this summer. You said he would help us," Mandie reminded her.

"Yes, he will do that," Sallie said. "As soon as we have time."

Joe and Uncle Ned came out of the house then, and Mandie noticed that they were wearing old clothes and carrying the ones they had had on. Uncle Ned hitched up his wagon so Sallie would have a way back home without Joe having to bring her back.

They traveled back to the slope and parked where they had before. This time Mandie carried Snowball with her when they went below to look for the mica. Uncle Ned was an expert in tracking anything. The others followed him as he found traces of the mica along the way.

Mandie smiled at Joe who kept rolling up the legs of the trousers he was wearing. Evidently they were made for Uncle Ned's long legs.

"They were the shortest ones he could find," Joe remarked, grinning at her.

"I hope you don't drown in them," Mandie replied with a laugh.

They had worked their way back to the river where Uncle Ned had brought them before.

"Now we look in water," the old man told Joe. He stepped out onto a large rock at the edge of the water.

Joe followed him, and the girls watched them as they stepped from boulder to boulder and waded in the water between. They bent down now and then and scooped up silt from the bottom where it was shallow. Uncle Ned closely examined each handful and stooped occasionally to peer into the water.

"I don't believe they are finding anything, or Joe would be yelling at us about it," Mandie said, letting Snowball down to walk at the end of his leash.

"No, there is no mica in the river," Sallie said. "I can see that my grandfather has not found any and he is puzzled."

Soon Uncle Ned and Joe gave up and returned

to the riverbank where the girls were waiting. They were both dripping wet and could hardly walk in the soaking wet clothes.

"No mica," Uncle Ned declared as they joined Mandie and Sallie.

"Let's go back to the cart so we can change into our dry clothes, Uncle Ned. It's not exactly warm enough today to go swimming," Joe remarked with chattering teeth and a big grin. He ran up the slope and the others followed.

As Uncle Ned and Joe retrieved their clothes from the wagon and the cart, Uncle Ned told the girls, "Sit in cart. We go back here, change clothes." He motioned to a thicket behind the place where they were parked.

Sallie and Mandie waited in the cart, and when Uncle Ned and Joe came back, they were dried off and wearing their clothes. They threw the wet clothes in the wagon. And to Mandie's surprise, Uncle Ned took a large basket from his wagon and brought it over to the cart.

"Now we eat," he said, stepping up into the cart.

Joe quickly followed, grinned at Mandie, and said, "Uncle Ned thinks of everything. I didn't remember to bring any food."

"I think time to eat," the old man said, opening the lid on the basket. He pulled out a folded tablecloth and spread it on the floor of the cart. Then he brought out the food—biscuits, fried chicken, corn on the cob, and baked potatoes.

"My goodness, Uncle Ned!" Mandie exclaimed as she watched. "Where did you get all this food in such a hurry?"

"Morning Star leave food," the old man said with a big smile.

"My grandmother cooked before she went off today because she knew my grandfather would be back," Sallie said, passing around tin plates from the basket.

Snowball went wild when he smelled the food. Uncle Ned picked the gizzard out of the bowl of chicken and handed it to Mandie. "Give white cat," he said.

Mandie took it and looked around. She didn't want Snowball to grease up the floor of the cart. Spotting a folded burlap bag in the back, she asked Joe, "Is it all right if I put this on that bag so Snowball won't drag it all over the place?"

"Go ahead," Joe agreed. "He won't hurt anything."

After the cat got his dinner and everyone had settled down with food, Uncle Ned told them, "Mica not here. Mica traveled downriver."

"But I thought y'all didn't find any mica in the river," Mandie said in surprise.

"No mica in river. Mica ride on raft or boat downriver," the old man explained.

Mandie's eyes opened wide and she said, "My goodness, it would take one of my grandmother's ships to haul all that mica down the river."

"Maybe some by river, some by wagon. Schoolman say wagons missing," Uncle Ned replied.

"Oh, I see," Mandie said. "But it sure would take a long time to move that mica by any means, wouldn't it, Joe?"

"Yes, that's what I told Uncle Ned. It was a huge pile," Joe agreed.

"We find missing wagons, we find missing mica," Uncle Ned insisted.

"So what do we do now?" Mandie asked between bites of fried chicken.

Uncle Ned paused from eating the corn off the cob and replied, "We look for wagons."

"Mr. O'Neal said he might join us later today, so maybe he will show up and help. This is going to be an awfully big job," Joe remarked, digging into a baked potato.

"We have done bigger jobs before," Sallie reminded him. She was also eating a piece of chicken.

Joe looked at the two girls, grinned, and said, "Here we go again!"

"We haven't found a mystery yet that we couldn't solve," Mandie reminded him. "It's just that we don't have a lot of time for this one, because I have to go home Saturday. We'll have to hurry."

Mandie began thinking of possibilities for the solution of this mystery.

Chapter 6 / The Stranger in the Woods

After they had consumed most of the food in the basket, Uncle Ned put the remaining food in a pouch with his bow and arrows. The young people waited for Uncle Ned's suggestions as to how to begin this search for the missing wagons as they all sat in the cart.

"Three wagons missing, three different parts of country," Uncle Ned told them. "Jessan live Deep Creek. Uncle Wirt live Bird-town. Dimar live up mountain betwixt. Take long time to steal from all three people. Take long time to hunt all three places." He paused to think.

"Uncle Ned, maybe we should split up and go in three different directions at one time. That way we'd get finished quicker," Mandie suggested, holding the end of Snowball's leash as he prowled around the inside of the cart.

"No, no, too dangerous. Must stay together. We nearer Dimar now. We go find Dimar," he spoke decisively, standing up and jumping down from the cart.

"Are we going in two different vehicles?" Joe asked as he, too, stood up and stepped down.

"No, only to Dimar house," Uncle Ned told him. "We leave cart with mother of Dimar."

Uncle Ned led the way up the mountain in his wagon. Joe, driving the cart, followed with the girls and Snowball. When they arrived at Dimar's house, they found Jerusha Walkingstick at her home, but her son, Dimar, was not there.

"Dimar gone look for wagon," Jerusha told them as they stood at the front door of her cabin in the mountain woods.

"We go look for wagons, too," Uncle Ned told her. "Dimar come home, tell him we search. Need him help."

"He went to look in woods by house of Uncle Wirt in Bird-town," the woman replied. "Not gone long."

"We go look by Uncle Wirt's house. Find Dimar maybe, too," the old man told her.

"Dimar told us your wagon was in the barn yesterday and then was not there last night," Sallie said. "Did anyone come this way yesterday?"

"No, no one I see," Jerusha replied.

"We leave cart here and go in wagon. Be back for it," Uncle Ned told her.

Jerusha nodded and said, "Leave cart front where I see."

Mandie spoke up. "What color shirt is Dimar wearing?"

Everyone looked surprised at that question.

Jerusha frowned as she replied, "Wear color brown shirt, with deerskin jacket."

"I wanted to know because we might be able to spot him at a distance in the woods by the color of his shirt," Mandie explained.

Joe smiled at her and said, "Yes, I remember how we were followed one time by someone in a white shirt, and we were able to identify him later by the shirt."

"We go now," the old man told the young people. He started down the front path and waved his hand back at Jerusha in the doorway.

Joe rushed to the cart and got his rifle, which he had brought from home. Everyone followed and scrambled into Uncle Ned's wagon. Joe had already tethered the horse and cart in view of the front door. Mandie held on to Snowball.

Uncle Ned usually drove at a slow pace but today he was in a hurry. He rushed over bumps and ruts in the dirt road, causing Mandie's teeth to chatter. She looked at her friends. They were also being shaken about as they clung to the side of the wagon. Joe was riding on the seat beside Uncle Ned and grasping the side rail. Sallie smiled at Mandie and held on with both hands as she sat on the floor of the wagon bed. And Snowball, with his leash tied to a hook on the rail, was loudly protesting as he looked at his mistress.

"One thing for sure, going at this speed we'll soon be at Uncle Wirt's house," Mandie said to Sallie over the rattle of the wagon.

Sallie smiled at her and agreed, "Yes."

When Uncle Ned pulled the wagon up into the front yard of Uncle Wirt's house, they were immediately surrounded by Mandie's Cherokee kinpeople. Her grandmother had been Uncle Wirt's sister and had died many years before Mandie was born, but these people knew Mandie and loved her as one of them.

"Welcome, my daughter," Uncle Wirt said, embracing Mandie as she stepped down from the wagon.

Mandie knew the Cherokee people did not classify kinpeople like the white people do. She was really Uncle Wirt's great-niece. And most of her relatives called each other brother or sister. It had been confusing for her to learn this, and even now she had to stop to think what the exact connection was with all these kinpeople.

"I love you, Uncle Wirt," Mandie said, standing on tiptoe to plant a kiss on the old man's cheek. Then she turned to his wife, Aunt Saphronia, and hugged her.

The little old woman probably had a million wrinkles that increased as she greeted Mandie with a big smile.

After everyone had been greeted in the yard, Uncle Wirt led the way into their log cabin. "Sit," he told them.

Uncle Ned remained standing and said, "We come, look for wagon. Look for Dimar to help."

"Yes, wagon leave barn. I not see," Uncle Wirt replied with a frown as he, too, stood nearby. "Dimar look, not find."

"Where is Dimar now, Uncle Wirt?" Mandie asked as she perched on a handmade chair.

"Dimar here this morning," Uncle Wirt explained. "Go up to woods. Look for three wagons. Puzzle. Not figure out." He shook his head and his long, silver-streaked hair swung about his face.

"We go find Dimar, help together," Uncle Ned replied.

The young people stood up as the old man turned back toward the front door.

"We do have to hurry because my mother expects Mandie and me back home for supper," Joe reminded everyone.

"Me go?" Uncle Wirt asked Uncle Ned as he pointed to his chest.

"No," Uncle Ned replied. "Stay here. Wait for Dimar. We go to woods, tell him. We not sure we find him, but we look for wagons in woods."

"Yes, we tell Dimar," Uncle Wirt agreed, and turning to Mandie he said, "Come back, see Cherokee kinpeople."

"As soon as I can, Uncle Wirt. I have to go home Saturday, but I'll be back when school gets out for the summer," Mandie promised.

The young people piled back into the wagon, and Uncle Ned headed toward the thick woods on the mountain. Mandie knew that at some point the wagon would not be able to get through the dense forest and that Uncle Ned would leave it parked somewhere and they would proceed on foot. She had been through many mysteries with the old man and was familiar with the fact that the countryside had very few roads that were passable for a wagon.

Shortly thereafter Uncle Ned pulled the wagon into a clearing among the thick chestnut trees. The road ahead didn't look wide enough for the wagon to pass through.

"Now we walk," he told the young people as he tethered the horse to a bush nearby.

Everyone jumped down. Mandie looked around. She could see an old log cabin through the trees above them and wondered if anyone lived there. Then Uncle Ned answered that question.

"Red Bird live up there. Know wagon, watch wagon," he said to the young people.

"Hadn't we better go tell him you're leaving it here?" Joe asked.

"No, he see. He see everything," the old man said, starting to climb a path in the opposite direction. "Now we walk, round, round, look at everything. Maybe see tracks from wagons." He was watching the ground as he walked. "Maybe see Dimar. All look." He glanced back at the young people.

Everyone immediately began watching the ground as they walked. Mandie had learned a little about tracking from the old man, and Sallie was an expert at it, but Joe had never been able to figure it all out. He would know a wagon wheel rut when he saw one, but he wouldn't know what kind of wagon or how fast it had been going.

"Joe, maybe you should just keep watching for a brown shirt and deerskin jacket as we walk through the woods," Mandie said as he walked by her side.

"That's a good idea. I can keep my rifle handy in case we run into trouble," Joe agreed. He put his rifle across his shoulder, straightened up, and kept looking in every direction as they proceeded up the mountain.

After a while the tiresome climb up the mountain ended on a level cliff of rock. Uncle Ned motioned for everyone to stand still.

"Now we see everywhere," he told them. He waved his hands around.

"I can see lots from up here, but where are we, Uncle Ned?" Joe asked.

"Almost to top of mountain. Then we go down other side," the old man explained. "Look now for wagons. Look for Dimar." He again motioned all around them as he turned.

At that moment a shot rang out through the woods. Everyone jumped.

"Down!" Uncle Ned told them as he quickly stooped down.

Mandie sat down on the rock and hugged Snowball tightly. He was about to act up, and she didn't want him making any sound that some enemy might hear. And she was sure that shot must have come from an enemy, although she had no idea as to what direction it had been fired from or how near it had come to them.

Joe knelt on the rock beside Uncle Ned and held his rifle ready. The old man drew an arrow out of his bag in case he needed to shoot with his bow.

Everyone was silent, even Snowball. Mandie couldn't hear another sound in the woods, and she wondered if the person who shot the rifle was silently creeping up on them. She was afraid and didn't want her friends to know it, so she rubbed her face on Snowball's white fur, which also kept him quiet.

After a few minutes, Uncle Ned looked at the young people and said, "No more shots. We go, but we keep ready, watch, listen, see anything moves in woods." He slowly stood up, balanced the pouch holding his bow and arrows on his shoulder, and all the time he kept watching the woods around them.

The young people silently followed him over the rock and up the last slope to the tip of the mountain, continuing to watch the ground for tracks. They didn't hear another sound.

Just as they reached the summit, another shot rang out, causing the three to stumble over each other as they tried to get down out of sight in the bushes nearby. Uncle Ned stooped down and readied his bow. This time he aimed and shot. Mandie could hear a singing sound as the arrow flew through the air into the woods beyond them.

"Did the shot come from the woods over there?" Joe asked. "Should I fire my rifle?"

"No, not yet," Uncle Ned answered as he kept looking in the direction his arrow had taken. "Enemy not know we have rifle. They come closer. We surprise them."

Joe silently agreed. He held his rifle ready.

"Look!" Mandie whispered, pointing above them. "I see someone in a white shirt up there."

Everyone looked in that direction. Joe turned his rifle that way. Uncle Ned squinted his black eyes and silently watched as the person with the white shirt slowly moved to their left on the crest of the hill.

They were too far away to be sure, but Mandie thought it was a man, a tall man at that and not very heavy, but she couldn't tell whether the person was white or Cherokee. While she was debating this in her mind, the person suddenly slipped and slid down some rocks.

Uncle Ned immediately jumped up and raced up the hill toward the person. Joe followed with his rifle.

Mandie looked at Sallie and asked, "Should we go, too?"

"No, we might get in their way. We stay here,"

Sallie said from where she had sat down on the ground.

Mandie, afraid to stand up, crawled over to her friend, holding the white cat's leash firmly in one hand. "Could you tell who it was?" she asked.

"Too far away," Sallie replied.

The girls watched as Uncle Ned and Joe overtook the person on the cliff. There was a scuffle during which Mandie held her breath, but then she could tell that Uncle Ned had succeeded in tying the person's hands behind their back. She breathed a sigh of relief.

Mandie and Sallie were so intent on watching the scene above, they were suddenly frightened speechless as someone approached them from behind.

Mandie instantly turned around and then burst into laughter. "It's Dimar!" she said, getting up to meet him as he came through the bushes.

Dimar was a tall, good-looking Cherokee boy, about Joe's age, and he had been Mandie's secret admirer from the first time he had seen her a long time ago. At least he thought he had kept it a secret, but Mandie knew every time she looked at him. And it made a problem for her because she believed Sallie was secretly interested in Dimar. And Sallie was her best Cherokee friend.

He reached for Mandie's hand, squeezed it, then did the same to Sallie's. "What are you girls doing here?" he asked.

They both tried to explain at once, and when he finally understood, he looked up the hill. Uncle Ned and Joe were bringing the person down toward them.

"Do you know who that is?" Mandie asked him

as the three continued watching.

"No, he is not Cherokee," Dimar replied, frowning.

As Uncle Ned and Joe got down to them, Mandie could see the man was white and probably not much older than Joe. He was wearing a white shirt and brown pants. Evidently he had been carrying a rifle because Uncle Ned now held a rifle in his hand.

When they finally approached the girls, Mandie could also see that the man's hands were tied behind him. She looked at Dimar to see if he recognized the man. He shook his head at her.

"This man shoot," Uncle Ned explained. "Say shoot for rabbit, but we say he shoot at us." He turned to Dimar and said, "Good we find you. Know this man?"

"No, Uncle Ned, I've never seen him before," Dimar replied. "But maybe he knows something about the stolen wagons."

Joe spoke up. "He said he would tell us what he knows if we will let him go. So we brought him down here to talk."

"What do you know about the wagons?" Dimar asked.

"I ain't had nuthin' to do with your wagons, or whatever it is that you've got missing," the man sputtered in anger as Joe kept his rifle pointed at him.

"Then how can you tell us something about the wagons?" Mandie asked.

The man quickly looked at her and said, "I ain't had nuthin' to do with stealin' no wagons."

"Then how do you know about the stolen wagons?" Dimar asked.

"I ran across this tall Injun man looking for stolen wagons back down the mountain," the man stuttered as he evidently tried to think of an answer that would be satisfactory.

"And who was this Indian man? Why did he talk to you about stolen wagons?" Dimar demanded.

"Said his name was something like Jessie, and said he lives at Deep Creek and someone stole his wagon and two more," the man told them.

"Jessan," Mandie said.

"Yes, Jessan's wagon was stolen," Dimar agreed. Looking at the man, he asked, "Where were you yesterday? And last night?"

"I walked over the mountain yesterday, and last night this here fella at some kind of schoolhouse or something that I came across let me sleep inside his building where he lived. I left before daylight and been walking ever since," the man told them.

"Riley O'Neal," Mandie said, looking around the group.

Everyone nodded in agreement.

"Where are you from? Where are you going?" Joe asked.

"I come from Tennessee. I'm on my way to Georgia," the man said.

"Why are you going to Georgia?" Mandie asked.

The man instantly turned his attention to her. He smiled and Mandie thought he was not bad looking and didn't look like a crook. Maybe he was not guilty of a crime.

"I'm looking for work. Can't find nuthin' to do in Tennessee and hear tell there's jobs on farms in Georgia," the man explained.

Mandie noticed that everyone was looking at everyone else. She was sure they were trying to decide what part of the man's story was true, because that's exactly what she was doing. And she felt he was telling the truth.

Finally Uncle Ned said, "You go on over mountain with us. Then we let you go on to Georgia. But must behave."

"I will. I promise," the man said, his blue eyes lighting up with relief.

Everyone looked at Uncle Ned as though to question his decision. The old man nodded and said, "White man not need three wagons. We let him go."

"I believe you are right, Uncle Ned," Dimar agreed. "Besides, whoever stole the wagons didn't even steal a single horse, so how could this man drive a wagon without a horse?"

"Thank you," the young man told Dimar. "I may be a bum, but I ain't no thief."

"Now, we take off rope but must keep walking with us. We have bow and arrow and rifles," Uncle Ned warned him as he walked over to untie the rope holding the man's hands.

"Thank you again," the man said, rubbing his wrists.

"You must have a name. What is it?" Mandie asked.

The man smiled at her again and said, "My name is Beethoven Jones."

Everyone laughed.

"I suppose you were named after the famous Beethoven," Mandie queried.

"Yes, my mother was a famous concert pianist in New York before she married my pa," the man explained.

"My grandmother is making me learn to play the piano at school, and I haven't decided whether

I like it or not," Mandie remarked as the group started moving ahead. Then she became aware of her friends' silent stares and decided to say no more.

Uncle Ned led the group up over the mountain. From there Mandie could see a road below winding through the trees. The old man pointed as he said to the man, "Here is your rifle. We trust you not shoot us."

"I wouldn't ever shoot anyone, mister, honest. Thank you," the man said, bowing as he took his rifle from Uncle Ned. "But I do need something to eat. Is it all right with you if I shoot a rabbit?"

Uncle Ned opened the pouch he had been carrying on his shoulder with his bow and arrows and pulled out the remains of the food they had had at noon. "Take," he told the man, holding it out to him wrapped in a napkin. "Better than rabbit. Cooked. Not raw."

The man was overwhelmed with Uncle Ned's kindness. He bent and kissed the old man's hand as he accepted the food. "Thank you, sir, thank you," Beethoven said, and looking toward the sky, he added, "And thank you, my dear Lord, for taking care of me."

Mandie felt tears rise in her eyes as she realized they had almost made a big mistake. The man certainly was not a criminal, and she was so glad they had the food to give him. She stepped forward, took the man's hand, and said, "I have a special verse that I always say when I'm in trouble or scared or worried, if you would like to use it, too."

"Oh certainly, miss," Beethoven told her.

"It goes like this, 'What time I am afraid, I will trust in thee.' And after you say it, you will feel better and everything will work out," she promised him.

" 'What time I am afraid, I will trust in thee,' " the man repeated. "Thank you again. I will always remember that."

The group stood there watching the man disappear down the side of the mountain, eating out of the napkin as he went. Mandie felt happy that they had done a good deed.

Chapter 7 / Where Is Mr. Smith?

After the stranger went on his way, Uncle Ned decided it was time for Mandie and Joe to return to the Woodards'. The sun was setting behind the mountain and darkness would soon come.

"Time you go home," Uncle Ned told Joe as they stood on the top of the mountain. "I take you back to get cart, then I go with Dimar to look more for wagons."

"I wish we could stay longer," Joe replied. "But I know my mother will be awfully put out if we don't get back in time for supper."

"Maybe we could meet up with y'all tomorrow and help look some more," Mandie said. Turning to Sallie, she asked, "Will you be at the school to-morrow?"

"No, I do not go tomorrow," Sallie said.

"I just thought about something," Joe told Uncle Ned. "Remember that Mr. O'Neal said he might meet up with us at the river. I wonder if he went and waited there?"

"Me and Dimar, we go see," Uncle Ned told him. "We take Sallie home first." He looked at Dimar and asked, "How you come to mountain?"

"My horse is tied up down by Red Bird's house, where you left your wagon," Dimar explained. "That's how I found you. Red Bird told me you came up this way."

"So Red Bird did see us," Mandie said, smiling at Uncle Ned.

"Yes, he always see," the old man agreed.

"Can we help look again tomorrow, Uncle Ned?" Mandie asked.

Uncle Ned nodded and said, "Meet at schoolhouse early. My house too far. I bring Sallie. Dimar come, too."

Everyone agreed, and they all went to Dimar's house to get Joe's cart. There they said good-bye, and Joe and Mandie headed for the Woodards' house.

"Do you think we'd have time to go by and see if Mr. Jacob Smith is home?" Mandie asked as they traveled down the road. Snowball was asleep in her lap.

"Sure, we can stop by for a minute," Joe agreed, loosely holding the reins as the horse pulled the cart.

They soon approached Mandie's father's house, where Mr. Smith lived, and Mandie said in disappointment, "I don't see any smoke coming out of the chimney. I'm afraid he's not home." She felt really frustrated. Where was Mr. Jacob Smith? Were they never going to catch him at home?

Joe turned the cart down the lane to the house.

"Let's look in the barn first to see if his horse is there," he said, halting the cart by the barn and jumping down.

Mandie held tightly to Snowball, who was awake now, stepped down, and followed Joe to the barn door. "No horse! Oh shucks!" The barn was empty.

"I don't understand why we can't catch up with him," Joe said, shaking his head as he turned to look at the house.

"Maybe he had some urgent business of some kind and had to go somewhere," Mandie suggested as she, too, gazed at the house. "I think we ought to go knock on the door just in case he is in the house and the horse is gone for some reason."

"Yes," Joe agreed.

They hurried over to the house and went up the front steps. Mandie knocked hard on the door. They listened but only silence greeted them.

"Maybe he has gone over to my house," Joe told Mandie. "He knew you were coming this week, so he could have gone to see if you were there."

"Then we'll soon find out," Mandie replied.

They went on down the road to Joe's house, and he drove the cart to the barn. Mandie jumped down and waited while he took care of the horse. Since it was suppertime, Joe put the horse in its stall for the night.

"I don't see my father's buggy, so he's not home yet," Joe remarked as he looked in the other corridors of the barn.

"We're not having much luck catching up with people today, are we?" Mandie said with a little laugh.

"Come on. At least my mother should be home," Joe said.

They hurried to the back door of the house and on into the kitchen. There they found Mrs. Miller, who was preparing supper.

"Well, I'm glad to see somebody will be here to eat supper," Mrs. Miller said as they shut the door behind them and began removing their wraps. Mandie set Snowball down, and he ran for the heat of the cookstove and sat down there, washing his face.

"My father hasn't come home yet, has he?" Joe said.

"No, not yet, and neither has your mother," Mrs. Miller replied as she stirred the contents of a pot on the stove.

"My mother is not here?" Joe asked. "Where did she go?"

"She went to a quilting bee down at Miss Abigail's right after noontime," Mrs. Miller told him. "Said she would be home in time for supper."

Mandie walked over to the stove and held her hands out to the warmth. "Who are they making a quilt for?" she asked.

"Some widow lady way over yonder on the other side of Bryson City," Mrs. Miller told her.

"Do you know if Mr. Jacob Smith has been by here today?" Joe asked as he joined Mandie by the stove.

"Not that I know of," Mrs. Miller said, lifting the lid to another pot. "I've been here all afternoon and have not seen hide nor hair of him."

"We've been by his house several times and he never is at home," Joe told her.

"According to what I hear, he is still traveling back to his house in the mountains," Mrs. Miller told him. She checked the roast in the oven. "Seems he has things up there that he's gradually moving down here."

"Mandie, maybe he just plain forgot that I told him on Friday that you were coming to visit," Joe said. "He must be gone back to his old house for something."

"I hope he gets back before I have to go home," Mandie replied. She glanced at Joe as they both stood by the warm cookstove, and she thought again about his farewell to her when he had gone away to college. She just had to ask him what he was trying to tell her as the train pulled out of the depot that day, but she had to pick the right moment to do this because she felt it might be something she didn't want anyone else to hear.

"Why so deep in thought?" Joe asked her, breaking through her memory.

Mandie shuffled her feet and said, "I was just thinking."

"I know. I could tell that from the expression on your face. It must have been some awfully serious thinking," Joe replied with a smile.

Mandie felt her face blush. She wouldn't meet Joe's gaze and looked across the room instead. "I doubt that it was anything serious," she said with a little nervous laugh.

"That's all right if you don't want to tell me what it was. I won't tell you what I was thinking when I looked at you either, then," Joe teased.

Mandie giggled and said, "Oh, so you were thinking, too."

Mrs. Miller had moved across the room to the cabinet and was taking down the dishes for the supper table. "Do you suppose y'all could stop doing all that thinking long enough to tell me whether y'all want to eat now or wait for Mrs. Woodard to come home? Goodness knows when the doctor will be back."

Mandie quickly looked at Joe and said, "I think I'd rather wait for your mother, so she can tell us all about that quilting bee."

Joe laughed and said, "All right, fine, but I don't imagine there's much to talk about concerning a quilting bee." Looking at Mrs. Miller, he said, "We'll just wait for my mother."

Mrs. Miller was setting the table as she replied, "Then I'll just keep everything warm."

At that moment the back door opened and Dr. Woodard came in. "Well, well, looks like I'm just in time for supper," he said, looking at the table and the young people standing by the stove.

"Yes, sir," Mrs. Miller said with a big smile. "I'm waiting for Mrs. Woodard. She ought to be here any minute now."

Dr. Woodard set down his medical bag and removed his coat and hat. He looked at Mrs. Miller and asked, "And where is Mrs. Woodard?"

"She's over at Miss Abigail's—" Mrs. Miller started to explain.

"At that quilting bee," the doctor interrupted. "Sorry, I forgot she told me about that this morning." He looked at Joe and asked, "And did y'all have a productive day?"

"Well, you see, we—" Joe began.

"Never mind," Dr. Woodard interrupted Joe this time. "Let me go get cleaned up, and I'll be right back to hear about it." He quickly picked up his things and left the room.

"Always in a hurry," Mrs. Miller remarked under her breath.

Joe heard her and said, "I wish he could take a day or two off now and then, but people just keep on getting sick and he keeps on doctoring them." He sighed loudly.

Mandie said, "That's exactly why I wouldn't want to marry a doctor." She grinned at Joe and added, "But who knows? I may never get married at all. I may be too busy with a career of my own to be a housewife." Suddenly realizing she shouldn't have said such a thing, because she knew Joe would immediately pick up on it, she quickly said, "Maybe your father knows where Mr. Jacob Smith is."

"Maybe," Joe agreed.

Mrs. Woodard came in the back door then with her sewing basket. "I hope I didn't keep supper waiting," she said to Mrs. Miller.

"No, ma'am," Mrs. Miller said. "The doctor just got home, and now that you are here, I'll have it all on the table right away."

Joe looked at his mother and asked, "We had your cart. How did you get to Miss Abigail's house?"

Mrs. Woodard began unbuttoning her coat as she walked on toward the door to the hallway. "Mrs. Amberson came by and got me, since she had to drive right by here anyway, and then she brought me back on her way home," she explained.

Looking at Mandie, she added, "I'll get rid of these things, and we'll talk about your day, Amanda, at supper."

"Yes, ma'am," Mandie said. "We had an interesting day."

When Mrs. Woodard returned to the kitchen a few minutes later, Dr. Woodard was with her, and everyone took their places at the supper table, which stood at one end of the long room. The Woodards had a dining room like the one Mandie was used to at home, but they only used it when they had lots of company, or in the summertime when the weather was warm enough that no fire had to be built in the huge stone fireplace and the heat from the iron cookstove was uncomfortable in the kitchen.

"Mrs. Miller, you take your food and go on home now and eat. I'm sure Mr. Miller must be waiting for his supper," Mrs. Woodard told the woman as she set the last dish on the table.

"Thank you, Mrs. Woodard. I'll be back by the time y'all finish and clear everything away," Mrs. Miller replied. She went to the stove and began filling dishes from the pots and putting them in a large wicker basket. It was understood that she cooked enough at every meal to have food to take home for her husband and herself.

As they began the meal, Dr. Woodard asked questions about their day's activities. "Did y'all figure out anything about that mica mound you found?"

"It's gone," Mandie told him.

"And we weren't able to find it," Joe added. "Not only that, did you know about the wagons that are missing?"

"Wagons missing?" Dr. Woodard asked, looking up from his plate.

Between them, Mandie and Joe explained about the missing wagons and Uncle Ned's decision that the wagons and the mica were connected.

"This may be a dangerous situation," Mrs. Woodard spoke up, looking at her husband.

"I can't see that there's any real danger in all this," Dr. Woodard told her, setting down his coffee cup. "It sounds more like a prank to me, someone moving all that mica about the countryside. And I'd say Uncle Ned is right in thinking the wagons are connected with it."

When the two young people told them about the stranger named Beethoven, whom they had met on the mountainside, Mrs. Woodard immediately looked at her husband again and said, "This stranger could have been a criminal."

Dr. Woodard shook his head and said, "No, not this particular man. I haven't seen him myself, but old Mrs. Montgomery was telling me that a stranger by that name had stayed at the Cherokee schoolhouse last night. Seems Riley O'Neal allowed him to sleep there."

Mandie and Joe looked at each other.

"That's what the man told us," Mandie said, laying down her fork.

"And we were going to check it out with Mr. O'Neal when we see him again," Joe added. He smiled as he swallowed the bite of meat in his mouth.

"So he was telling the truth," Mandie said.

"We'll have to tell this to Uncle Ned in the morning," Joe said.

"I don't think y'all should go around talking to strangers unless Uncle Ned, or some other adult, is with y'all," Mrs. Woodard told them.

"We're supposed to meet Uncle Ned and Sallie and Dimar at the Cherokee schoolhouse tomorrow morning to continue searching for the wagons," Joe said.

"And looking for the mica," Mandie added.

Looking at his mother, Joe asked, "Will you be needing your cart tomorrow? Or are you finished with the quilting?"

"You go ahead and take it. Mrs. Amberson has promised to stop by and pick me up on her way back to Miss Abigail's tomorrow morning," Mrs. Woodard told him. "We'll probably have another week or two of working on the quilt, but while Amanda is here it's easier for y'all to get about using the cart."

"Thank you, Mother," Joe told her.

"I appreciate your thoughtfulness, Mrs. Woodard," Mandie said, then she realized she was sounding like one of the Misses Heathwood's young ladies. She wondered if the school was going to change the way she acted and talked. Was it getting to be a habit? She wasn't sure she wanted to change, so she added, "It sure is nice to visit back here in the country. I don't have to act so proper. I can just be me, Mandie Shaw." She smiled at Mrs. Woodard.

"Oh, you will always be you, Amanda, no matter where you go to school or where you live. You're just a dyed in the wool country girl," Mrs. Woodard replied, sipping her coffee.

"That's right," Dr. Woodard agreed, taking a biscuit from the platter in front of him. "I've always heard that you can take the girl out of the country, but you can't take the country out of the girl."

Mandie and Joe both laughed.

Mrs. Woodard told Dr. Woodard, "No, no, it's the boy the old saying is about, not a girl."

"Well, anyhow, I think it would apply to Miss Amanda," the doctor said with a smile for his wife. Looking at Mandie, he added, "I can't imagine Miss

Amanda ever turning into a real city girl."

In order to change the subject, Mandie asked, "Dr. Woodard, have you seen Mr. Jacob Smith today? We went by his house again—this morning and late this afternoon—and he wasn't home."

"No, I didn't see him today," Dr. Woodard told her.

"Mrs. Miller said he was going back to his old house now and then to haul some of his things down here," Joe said. "Do you suppose that's where he is?"

Mrs. Woodard frowned as she looked at Joe and said, "You know, Miss Abigail was wondering where he is, too. She said he borrows her cart to haul his belongings down here, since he doesn't even have a wagon yet. He was supposed to come by yesterday and get her cart, but he never showed up."

"Maybe he didn't need the cart," Dr. Woodard suggested.

"No, he definitely needed Miss Abigail's cart," Mrs. Woodard explained. "He had told her he was going to bring a huge trunk down from the old house. He's afraid the place might be ransacked if people up there find out he's no longer living there."

"Oh shucks," Mandie said with a slight frown. "Do you mean we have to go searching for Mr. Smith, on top of looking for the wagons, and also the mica? This is getting to be a complicated mystery."

"Yes, it is, and you love it," Joe teased.

"I don't know exactly how y'all are going to look for Mr. Smith when no one has any idea as to where he has gone," Mrs. Woodard told them.

"I'll ask on my rounds tomorrow if anyone has seen Mr. Smith. I'll be traveling in the direction he would take to his old house, but of course I won't be going that far," Dr. Woodard said, laying his fork down and looking across the room. "Now, I do believe I see a chocolate cake over there on the sideboard." He turned to grin at Mandie.

"I believe I do, too," Mandie agreed, grinning back as she looked in that direction.

"Well, I know for sure there's a chocolate cake over there on the sideboard," Joe said with a laugh.

"Since you are so sure there's a chocolate cake over there, why don't you just go get it and bring it to the table? I'll get rid of the plates," Mrs. Woodard said, rising and beginning to remove the dinner plates.

Mandie quickly stood and helped take the dirty dishes to the sink. Snowball had remained asleep on the woodbox by the stove until Mandie bent to put some scraps on his plate. Then he quickly woke up and without bothering to stretch or wash his face, he came bounding to see what was there.

"Now, don't drag it out onto the floor," Mandie told him. "Maybe I should stay right here and see that you don't."

"No, Amanda, let him be and come on back to the table," Mrs. Woodard said as she began slicing the cake that Joe had set in front of her and putting the slices in the the cake plates already on the table.

"You'd better hurry before I eat it all up," Joe warned her.

"Impossible," Mandie declared as she slipped back into her chair at the table.

They sat around the table eating cake and talking until Mrs. Miller returned. Then they went into the parlor.

Dr. Woodard settled down next to a lamp and

began reading a medical journal. Mrs. Woodard sat near another lamp with her Bible. She had told Mandie that she was in the process of reading straight through the book, and it was going to take some time to do that.

As Mandie and Joe sat on low stools by the fireplace, she said, "I suppose we could go back early in the morning to see if Mr. Smith is home, and if he's not, we could stop by and ask Miss Abigail if he ever came to get her cart."

"That's exactly what I was thinking," Joe told her. "It is strange that no one has seen him and no one knows where he went."

Mandie had a sudden idea. "You don't think he could be involved in the mica mystery, do you?" she asked.

"The mica?" Joe repeated. "No, I doubt that he would be because, for one thing, Uncle Ned thinks the stolen wagons are connected with the mica. I can't see Mr. Smith stealing wagons, much less moving a mound of mica."

With a sigh, Mandie agreed, "You're right. He was my father's friend, and I don't think he would be stealing anything. But I do wish we could find him."

"We will sooner or later," Joe promised.

"Well, I hope it's sooner than later," Mandie replied with a little laugh. "I would like to see him before I have to go home."

After she went to bed that night, Mandie thought about Mr. Jacob Smith for a long time. Where had he gone? Why had no one seen him? He wouldn't have just pulled up stakes and left the country. After all, he had restored her father's house and was living in it to take care of it until someday in the future when she would decide what to do with it.

There was something strange about the whole situation.

Chapter 8 / Separated in the Mountain

The next morning Mandie and Joe took Mrs. Woodard's cart and rode by to see if Mr. Jacob Smith was home. But the place was still deserted, so they went on by Miss Abigail's house.

Miss Abigail was sweeping off her front porch when Joe stopped the cart in her driveway. "My, my! Y'all are sure up early this morning," the lady greeted them with a smile.

"Yes, ma'am," Joe said as he jumped down from the cart. "We are looking for Mr. Jacob Smith, and my mother said he usually borrows your cart to haul things from his old house. We wanted to find out if he has been by to get it."

"Why, no. I was saying yesterday that he was supposed to come and get it on Monday, but he never did show up," Miss Abigail replied, stopping to lean on a post by the walkway. "Today's Wednesday, and I still haven't seen or heard from him."

"In case he does come by, Miss Abigail, would you please tell him I've been trying to find him?" Mandie asked as she remained seated in the cart. "I have to go home Saturday, and I want to see him before I leave."

"Of course, Amanda," Miss Abigail replied. "I'll ask around to see if anyone knows where he is, and I'll let you know if I learn anything."

"Thank you, Miss Abigail, and we'll let you know if we catch up with him," Mandie promised.

They continued on their way to the Cherokee schoolhouse. Mandie held firmly to Snowball's leash as he curled up in her lap. When Joe turned the cart into the school yard, Mandie saw Uncle Ned's wagon and Dimar's horse tied up under a tree, but no one was in sight.

"They must all be inside the schoolhouse," Joe said as he brought the cart to a stop next to the wagon.

"Yes, let's go see," Mandie replied as she held Snowball and jumped down. She started toward the front door, and Joe quickly followed.

"Good morning," Sallie called to them as she came to the open doorway.

Mandie and Joe returned the greeting as they came up to the porch.

"Have y'all been here long?" Mandie asked. She set Snowball down to walk and held his leash tightly as they entered the schoolroom.

"We just arrived," Sallie replied.

Uncle Ned and Dimar were seated in the back of the schoolroom talking with Riley O'Neal.

"Good morning," Mandie said as she looked at

the three. "Did y'all find out anything after we left yesterday?"

Uncle Ned and Dimar shook their heads in the negative.

"No, nothing," the old man said.

"Not a thing," Dimar added, smiling at Mandie.

Riley O'Neal spoke up. "They didn't find anyone or the wagons, but I did confirm for them that the man called Beethoven spent the night here at the schoolhouse. He seemed harmless and in dire need of something to eat and a place to sleep."

"I didn't think he looked dangerous," Mandie said, sitting down next to Uncle Ned on the bench. "In fact, I thought he looked humble."

"I believe you are a good judge of people, Miss Amanda," Riley O'Neal told her, smiling as he leaned forward from his seat on the other side of Uncle Ned.

Joe and Sallie sat down next to Dimar on the other bench.

"What are you planning to do today, Uncle Ned?" Joe asked.

"We look more," the old man replied. "Six of us now. We split and go two ways."

"Six?" Mandie questioned. She looked at Riley O'Neal and said, "Then you must be planning on going with us."

"No school today, so I thought I might be able to help in the search," Mr. O'Neal said.

"No school? But today's Wednesday. Don't the Cherokee children go to school every day during the week like we do?" Mandie asked.

"No, we are not full time yet," Riley O'Neal explained. "You see, the Cherokee children have to get used to the idea of going to school every day, so I am gradually adding one more day to the week. So far we are up to three days—Monday, Tuesday, and Thursday."

"Well, I wish I went to that kind of school," Mandie replied with a laugh.

"It sure would take you a long time to get educated," Joe teased.

"And you would be old before you finished enough school to get into college," Sallie reminded her.

"Oh shucks, I didn't really mean that. In fact, I'd like to go to school seven days a week and get it all over with in a hurry," Mandie replied.

"We go now," Uncle Ned said, standing up and smiling at Mandie as he added, "And get it over with in hurry."

"Yes, sir," Mandie agreed.

As they walked across the yard, Uncle Ned turned to look at them and said, "We go to mountain bottom," and then pointing to each one he added, "There we split. Me take Sallie, Mr. Schoolteacher, and Dimar take Mandie and Joe."

"Do we take the cart?" Joe asked.

"Yes," Uncle Ned replied. "Take cart. We take wagon."

As Mandie climbed into the cart with Dimar and Joe, she said, "I suppose you know which way to go from there, Dimar?"

Dimar looked at Mandie and Joe and explained, "He is dividing us this way because he and I know the trails. We will leave the wagon and the cart at the bottom of the mountain."

Mandie noticed that Dimar had his rifle with him, as did Joe, so she felt well protected. She sat between the boys on the seat, and Snowball decided he wanted to lie down on the floor, but Mandie held tightly to the end of his leash.

They followed Uncle Ned to the valley below the mountain where the old man pulled his wagon to a stop. He looped the reins loosely to a bush, giving his horse plenty of slack to graze. Joe tied up his horse and cart nearby. The area was full of young trees with new springtime leaves that provided the horses with plenty of shade in case the sunshine warmed up the valley before they returned.

Mandie jumped down from the cart, holding Snowball in her arms.

"Are you taking that cat with you? We have to climb up the mountain, you know," Joe said.

"Well, I can't leave him here," Mandie replied, stopping to look at Joe.

Dimar spoke behind her. "No, you cannot leave him here. He might get loose, or someone might come by and let him loose."

"That might not be such a bad thing to happen," Joe teased Mandie as they hurried over to where the others were waiting.

"Then you would have to help me find him," Mandie told him.

Uncle Ned explained his plans. "You go that trail." He pointed to a dense path leading up the mountain on his left. "We go that trail." He indicated another faint trail to the right.

Mandie thought about what he was saying and asked, "Then how do we get back together again, Uncle Ned?"

"Sun straight up we come back, eat," the old man told her.

"Eat?" Joe asked. "Mandie, we forgot to bring any food."

Uncle Ned smiled at him and said, "Morning Star make plenty food in wagon for all."

"Thank you, Uncle Ned," Mandie said. "I was about to say we ought to rush back to Joe's house and ask Mrs. Miller for something to eat later."

Riley O'Neal looked at Mandie and said, "I'm not used to such outings, so I didn't bring any food, either." Turning to Uncle Ned, he said, "Please tell Morning Star I am grateful she remembered to send food."

Uncle Ned nodded and started off to the right. "Go now," he said.

Sallie paused as she followed her grandfather and told Mandie, "I would help you carry Snowball but my grandfather is sending us in two different directions."

"Thank you, Sallie, but he won't be that much of a problem," Mandie replied. She hurried to catch up with Joe and Dimar.

The trail was steep in places, and Mandie found it was a struggle to hold on to Snowball and grasp bushes along the way to keep from sliding backward. Joe and Dimar both offered to help carry the cat, but Mandie knew it was her responsibility and she wouldn't dare admit she wished now she had left Snowball at the Woodards' house.

Dimar was in the lead and turned to say, "We searched this side of the mountain yesterday. We will search the other side after we go over the top."

"Going down the other side will probably be easier than all this climbing," Joe said.

"The other side is steep, too steep for my horse," Dimar said. "I have been there many times before. I always leave my horse below."

"Dimar," Mandie said, stepping closer as the

three of them stood on a large rock jutting out of the side of the mountain. "What exactly are we supposed to be looking for in this mountain?"

"Wagons, mica, people—anything that does not belong to the mountain," Dimar explained.

"And what do we do if we suddenly come upon someone?" Mandie asked.

Dimar touched his rifle over his shoulder. "We ask questions," he said. "However, we are prepared for more."

"Yes," Joe agreed, lifting his rifle.

"I have been thinking I should get myself a rifle," Mandie told the boys with a serious expression.

Joe smiled at her and said, "You wouldn't know what to do with it if you had a rifle."

Mandie frowned and said, "I could learn to shoot it."

"Yes," Dimar agreed. "I could teach you how."

Joe quickly said, "I could teach you how, too, but you don't have to get a rifle. I can take care of you."

"But what about when you aren't with me?" Mandie asked.

Dimar quickly said, "Get a rifle. I will teach you how to shoot it. Now we must go on." He began climbing the trail again.

As Mandie followed the boys, she thought about her father. She was sure he had had a rifle, and she wondered if it was still in the house where Mr. Jacob Smith lived now. If she could ever catch up with Mr. Smith, she would ask him about it.

After what seemed hours to Mandie, they finally reached the crest of the mountain. Dimar led the way to a small clearing where they flopped down in the grass to rest. Mandie let Snowball play at the end of his leash.

"Five minutes," Dimar told Mandie and Joe. "Then we go down the other side."

"How far are we going? Uncle Ned said to come back to his wagon at noontime," Mandie told Dimar.

"It will not take long to go down the mountainside, and then I know a shortcut to the wagon," Dimar explained. "But we have to watch and search as we go down."

"If Uncle Ned finds anything, or anybody, on his trail, how will we know?" Joe asked, stretching out in the grass.

"He will send a smoke signal. If we find anything, we will send him a smoke signal," Dimar explained.

"I haven't been looking up or watching the sky. Do you think we will see it if he does send one?" Mandie asked, pulling on Snowball's leash as he tried to break free.

"Yes, I have been watching," Dimar replied with a smile. He stood and motioned around him. "Look, you can see everywhere from here."

Mandie rose and looked around as she held Snowball's leash. She could see several lower peaks with valleys in between. Evidently they were on the highest part of the mountain. She wondered where Uncle Ned and the others were in all that landscape.

"The trail we came up was at an angle and not straight. We began down that way," Dimar explained, pointing down to his left.

Joe stood up and joined them. "There is one question I have," he said. "Suppose Uncle Ned runs into trouble somewhere and is not able to send us a message? How will we know that?"

"Uncle Ned is fast. He will send us a message somehow," Dimar told him. "Now we must go on."

Mandie picked up Snowball, and they started down the other side of the mountain. She found it was no easier going down than coming up. The small rocks under her feet seemed to roll and make her skid, causing Snowball to growl and want down. She tried walking him with his leash, but he kept sliding and she had to pick him up again.

Dimar, in the lead, kept looking all around them, and Mandie watched him for signs of anything he might see. Joe came down the trail behind her.

Since it was impossible to talk as they walked, Mandie had lots of time to think. She remembered that Uncle Ned had said at least part of the mica seemed to have been moved down the river, but they weren't even near the river that she could see. And she couldn't imagine how anyone could get a wagon on this mountain, so Uncle Ned must be looking for the people who moved the mica and who probably stole the wagons. But why would the people who stole the wagons leave them somewhere and then come to the mountain? So far she had not seen any sign of anyone living on the mountain—there were no houses of any kind and there was nothing but wilderness. But she knew Uncle Ned was always right in his decisions concerning mysteries.

Eventually the trail began leveling out and turning in a curve to their left.

"This will take us back to the wagon," Dimar explained as they finally reached flat ground again and were able to walk side by side and talk.

"So what good did it do to go up that mountain?" Mandie asked.

Dimar looked down at her with a smile. "To be sure no one was hiding up in the mountain," he said. "Next we will search the river."

"After we eat, I hope," Joe said.

"Yes, we will eat while Uncle Ned makes plans for us to follow this afternoon," Dimar said.

When they came within sight of the wagon, horses, and cart, Mandie said, "I don't see anyone. The others must not be back down yet."

"They had a longer trail to go," Dimar explained. "We will wait for them before we eat."

"I guess we'd better wait for them since Uncle Ned brought the food," Mandie said with a little laugh.

"My mother also sent food," Dimar told her. "I had given it to Uncle Ned to carry in his wagon."

"Well, in that case we could go ahead and eat what you brought, if Uncle Ned and Sallie and Mr. O'Neal don't hurry up and get back," Joe said with a grin.

"Joe, that wouldn't be nice," Mandie rebuked him as they approached the vehicles and horses. "I think I'd rather rest a few minutes before I eat." She sat down on the grass in the shade. "It feels warm down here after being up on that mountain."

"There is a spring a few paces down that pathway if you would like water," Dimar told her, motioning into the woods.

"Water?" Mandie said, sitting up. "Yes, I would really like some water." She stood up, holding on to Snowball's leash.

"I have a pail and some cups in the cart," Joe told her. "My mother insists they stay in the cart all the time for any unexpected emergencies, and I'd say this is one. I'll get them." He walked over to the cart and stepped into it.

"What about the horses? Shouldn't we take them to the water?" Mandie asked Dimar.

"Yes, after we eat we will water the horses," he told her.

Joe came back with the pail and cups. "I could go fill this up and bring it back up here," he told them.

"I want to go with you," Mandie said.

"I will stay here to watch for Uncle Ned," Dimar told them.

"We won't be gone long, and I'll bring a bucket-ful back for you," Joe promised.

Mandie picked up Snowball and followed Joe down the path. Just a few yards inside the cluster of trees they found the spring. The crystal-clear water was ice cold to the touch when Mandie stuck her finger into it. Snowball struggled to get to the water, and Mandie held his leash tight enough to keep him from walking into it. He growled as he licked the water.

Joe filled the pail and washed out the cups. Mandie took a cup from him, filled it, and drank almost all of the water in one long swallow. She coughed and shivered.

"That was colder than I thought it would be," she sputtered as she breathed deeply to inhale warm air.

"Glad you warned me. I'll wait and drink after we get back to the wagons," Joe said.

They rejoined Dimar and sat in the grass, drinking the cold water as they waited for Uncle Ned, Sallie, and Riley O'Neal to return. The three talked about various things, but Mandie kept wondering when the others would return. It had been an awfully long time since they had come back, and the others should not have been far behind them.

"Dimar, don't you think all the others should have been back by now?" Mandie finally asked.

"Yes, they should have been back," he agreed. "They may have had some problems somewhere."

"Problems?" Mandie asked. "You mean trouble?"

Dimar quickly looked at her and said, "No bad trouble. Uncle Ned would have signaled to us."

"But he might not have been able to," Mandie replied, a feeling of worry enveloping her.

"Maybe we should go look for them," Joe suggested.

"No, we do not know which way they are coming back," Dimar replied.

"Which way?" Mandie asked. "There is more than one way to come back down here?"

"Yes, several different paths," Dimar replied. "But do not worry. Uncle Ned will get himself and the others back without any trouble."

No matter how reassuring Dimar tried to be, Mandie was beginning to really worry about her friends. What if someone had managed to capture all of them? They wouldn't be able to send a message back. She didn't know how much longer she could wait, but what could she do? Dimar seemed so confident about the situation. Therefore, she wouldn't be able to talk him into going to look for them. She decided she would wait awhile longer, and then she would go by herself if the boys didn't want to accompany her. She had to find her friends because she had a feeling they were in trouble.

Chapter 9 / The Long, Long Trail

After what seemed like an hour of waiting for the others to return, Dimar stood up and said, "I will get the food my mother sent and we will eat." He started toward Uncle Ned's wagon, which was nearby.

"That sounds like a good idea," Joe agreed, rising to follow him.

Mandie walked Snowball on his leash and said, "Dimar, if the others haven't come back by the time we eat, do you think we could go look somewhere for them? We could leave a note here in case they come back and we miss them." She watched as Dimar and Joe brought a pail and a blanket from the wagon.

"Perhaps they will return before we finish eating," Dimar replied, stooping to spread the blanket on the grass. "If they have not, then we will go search for them." He looked up and smiled at Mandie.

"That is a good decision. We can't just sit here all day waiting," Joe told him as he helped smooth out the blanket.

"Thank you, Dimar," Mandie said. "What can I do to help?"

"Help eat," Dimar said, smiling again as he reached for the pail that Joe had set down.

Mandie watched as Dimar spread a small cloth over the center of the blanket and began taking biscuits out of the pail and laying them on it.

"My mother only sent biscuits, but you will find sausage in some and ham in others, and also some apples," Dimar explained.

"Oh, that sounds just right," Mandie said, sitting on the edge of the blanket.

Joe carried the pail of water that they had filled earlier over to the spread and set it down along with the cups. "Somebody might want some water," he said.

The three sat there and ate quickly. Even Snowball gobbled down the bits of food Mandie gave him. Everyone was so wound up with the suspense that no one had much to say.

Mandie looked at the boys and said, "I guess we're all on pins and needles, aren't we?"

Dimar quickly returned her look. "Pins and needles?" he asked.

Mandie smiled at him, remembering he was full-blooded Cherokee and probably didn't know all the white people's expressions. "Well, not real pins and needles," she tried to explain. "That means we can't sit still for wanting to go do something and solve the problem."

Dimar gave her a big smile and said, "I think I understand. Imaginary pins and needles are sticking you to urge you to do something."

Joe laughed and said, "I don't feel anything sticking me."

"I feel lots of them," Mandie said, laughing.

As soon as they finished eating and returned everything to Uncle Ned's wagon, Dimar told them, "We will go up the trail they took and look for markings and follow them. Then we will be sure we are on the same path they went."

"You mean bent twigs, pieces of broken vines, and all that, like Uncle Ned taught me to mark a path," Mandie said, carrying Snowball, who now wanted to run off.

"Yes," Dimar agreed. Picking up his rifle, he slung it over his shoulder and led the way toward the trail the others had gone up the mountain.

Mandie followed, holding tightly to her white cat, and Joe brought up the rear with his rifle.

As soon as they started up the trail, they found markings. Being careful not to disturb anything, they walked single file up the mountain. Coming out on a level clearing, Dimar quickly stooped to inspect the ground, motioning for Mandie and Joe to halt.

Mandie bent to watch. "You are looking for tracks to see if anyone else besides them was there, right?" Mandie asked, preventing Snowball from jumping down.

"Yes, and also to see which direction they went," Dimar explained carefully. "We must do this before we walk here and disturb their footprints," he added.

Joe removed his rifle from his shoulder and asked, "Would it do any good if we fired a shot?"

Dimar quickly stood up and said, "No, no, that

would not do. Anyone we are pursuing would be alerted by a shot. Uncle Ned said no shots except in trouble."

"You are right," Joe replied.

Dimar moved forward, still looking at the ground. "They went this way," he said. He slowly moved to the left and continued up the trail, carefully watching for tracks and markings.

Mandie stayed close behind him and noticed markings as he discovered them. Footprints were not distinct in the hard, rocky pathway, but Dimar seemed to be able to spot them. She looked back at Joe and saw that he was also searching for clues as they went.

Halfway up the mountain they came to a split in the trail. Dimar quickly examined the trail going off to the left and found tracks. Stooping to look closely, he said, "These tracks do not belong to Uncle Ned. They must have been made by Mr. O'Neal." Moving back to the fork, he inspected the trail to the right. "These are Uncle Ned's tracks . . . and also Sallie's." He stood up, looking puzzled as he glanced around.

"I wonder why Mr. O'Neal went off one way and Uncle Ned and Sallie went the other," Mandie said, frowning as she glanced up both trails from where she stood at the fork.

"I can see bent twigs up both paths," Joe remarked, squinting ahead.

"Yes," Dimar agreed.

"Do you know where these trails go? Have you been up them before?" Mandie asked the Cherokee boy.

"Yes, they come back together near the top of the mountain," Dimar replied.

"Why would they split up, especially sending Mr. O'Neal off on a trail by himself? He probably got lost or something. He's from up north, you know, and doesn't know about things like this," Joe said.

Dimar turned to smile at Joe and said, "He is a fast learner. Uncle Ned has taught him many things. Mr. O'Neal even knows how to shoot a rifle."

"I'm glad he does. He might need to use one up here in these woods," Mandie said. She let Snowball down to walk at the end of his leash.

"So what are we going to do? Split up, too?"

"Yes, that is necessary to cover both trails," Dimar told him. Turning to Mandie, he said, "You know how to look for markings on a trail. Do you want to go with Joe up one path and I will take the other one? We will meet at the top."

"All right," Mandie agreed. "I'm not real good at finding markings, but between Joe and me I think we'll be able to find the clues."

"You are one-fourth Cherokee. You will see everything," Dimar said, smiling at her as he put his rifle across his shoulder and turned to the path at the right. "I will go up this one. I remember that it is longer because it winds around in places. Wait for me at the top."

"If you get there first, wait for us," Mandie called to him as she and Joe started up the trail to the left. She stooped to pick up Snowball. It would be better to carry him so he wouldn't disturb any footprints along the way.

Mandie and Joe carefully walked to one side, following Mr. O'Neal's footprints. They kept watching for bent twigs and markings but found none until they were a long way up the trail.

"There's a broken branch on that bush," Mandie

said, pointing ahead to a limb hanging half off a small holly tree. She hurried to look at it as Joe followed her.

"Mandie, this looks like an old break," he said, examining the limb. "See the leaves are beginning to turn brown."

Mandie looked closer as she put Snowball down and held on to his leash. "But, Joe, the joint where it was broken looks fresh. It's still green," she told him.

"You're right," Joe agreed. He fanned through the sticky leaves. "The leaves must have been damaged somehow before. Do you think Mr. O'Neal broke the limb to mark his way?"

Mandie stooped to look at the ground. "He at least stopped here. See the footprints where he moved around a little bit, and then they go on up the trail," she said. Snowball meowed in protest as she squeezed him.

"So we go on up the trail," Joe agreed.

"Right," Mandie said, turning to look at Joe. "You know, it has been so long since we all started up the two trails this morning that I imagine Uncle Ned, Sallie, and Mr. O'Neal are a long way from here and we'll never be able to catch up with them."

"But, Mandie, we don't know where they went yet," Joe reminded her. "They might have seen someone or something and left the trail for another one way up ahead somewhere."

"Oh shucks!" Mandie said loudly as she stomped her foot. "This whole thing is so mixed up. I don't think we should have separated. There are so many possible complications that we may never find them. Then we would have to go back and sit by the wagon to wait for them to show up."

"If we don't find them, they will return to the wagon sooner or later," Joe told her. "Come on. Let's go. We haven't even made a good start yet."

"Oh well!" Mandie said with a loud sigh.

The two continued on up the trail and found Riley O'Neal's footprints all along the way. But there were no bent twigs or any signs of marking. Mandie silently decided Riley O'Neal didn't know how to do such a thing, regardless of what Dimar had said about Uncle Ned teaching Riley all these things. She was bored with the whole business. This was not the way she would go about solving the mystery of the stolen wagons and the mica mound that had disappeared, and she wondered why Uncle Ned was doing his investigation this way.

Snowball was tired of being carried. He wriggled in Mandie's arms and tried to escape.

"Snowball, be still!" Mandie commanded as she tightened her hold on the white cat, stopping to hold him up and look into his blue eyes. "You can't get down," she added.

Joe had walked on up the other edge of the trail and Mandie hurried to catch up with him. When she got alongside him on her side of the trail, Joe was slowly investigating the dirt, looking for footprints.

"Let's go faster, Joe, so we can hurry and get to the top," she told him as she, too, looked at the trail for signs. "We're supposed to meet Dimar up there, and then I suppose we'll have to work our way down the other side of the mountain. By that time Uncle Ned and Sallie and Mr. O'Neal may be waiting for us at the wagons."

"I'm willing to go faster, but how about you? This is awfully steep terrain and pretty hard to walk up in some places," Joe reminded her, straightening up.

Mandie grinned at him and said, "I can make it if you can." She moved Snowball's weight from one arm to the other.

"Even with that cat? I know he's heavy. Why don't you let me carry him?" he offered.

"I'll just put him down to walk at the end of his leash in places where the ground is level enough, but, you know, cats can climb, so maybe I'll just let him trail along and do his own climbing," Mandie replied.

"Please don't let him get away. That's all we need to slow us up," Joe reminded her.

Mandie knew Snowball had a habit of running away whenever he got a chance, but she was tired of being reminded of it. "If he manages to run away, I'll go after him. You won't have to bother with it," she said as she set the white cat down and held tightly to his leash.

Joe looked at her and frowned but didn't say anything. He started on up the trail.

Mandie felt sorry for her snappy remark but turned her attention to the cat and proceeded along the way. Snowball was delighted to have the run of the leash and he inspected everything they passed.

There were no trail markings that they could see, only the footprints belonging to Mr. O'Neal, and they reached the top of the mountain quicker than they expected. Dimar was already there, sitting on a stump and waiting for them.

"You must have worked awfully fast," Mandie said, catching her breath and flopping down on a nearby boulder as she held Snowball's leash. She looked out over the valley, hoping to see some sign of her other friends, but there was no one else in sight.

"I am more experienced than you and Joe are," Dimar said with a big smile. "I only found Uncle Ned's and Sallie's prints, but they did leave a lot of markings along the way."

"We didn't find anything but Mr. O'Neal's footprints," Joe told him as he sat down on a fallen log nearby.

"Dimar, this is taking an awfully long time," Mandie said with a big sigh. "Couldn't we do something a little faster?"

"It will be faster going downhill than it was coming up," Dimar reminded her. "There are two valleys between here and the foot of the mountain, and we will have a better view of our surroundings. But, alas, there are several trails. I hope Uncle Ned, Sallie, and Mr. O'Neal all went down the same pathway." He stood up and stretched.

"So do I," Mandie agreed.

"Have you seen any sign of anyone else? Any other prints, that is?" Joe asked. He rose and picked up his rifle.

"Nothing," Dimar replied.

"So we are probably wasting all this time for nothing," Mandie said, standing up to tighten her hold on Snowball's leash as he tugged to run away.

"No, not for nothing," Dimar told her. "We have to investigate all possibilities until we come to the right one."

"Dimar, whoever stole those wagons couldn't possibly bring them up this mountain," Mandie told him.

"It is possible on certain trails to get a wagon up

the mountain if someone knew how to do this," Dimar replied.

"In other words, it would have to be Cherokee people to figure that out," Joe said.

"Yes," Dimar replied. "This mountain is no mystery to the Cherokee people, only to the white people."

"Then you believe whoever stole the wagons and moved the mica were Cherokee people," Mandie said, frowning as she thought about this.

"Yes, and Uncle Ned also believes this," the Indian boy said. "That is why we are searching this mountain. He thinks we will find their trail somewhere near here."

"I hope we do soon," Mandie said as the three of them continued on the trail.

Dimar was right. There were valleys now and then and a clear view, but they saw nothing suspicious and didn't meet up with anyone. Now and then the mountainside seemed to drop straight down, and it was in one of these places that Mandie suddenly slid on loose rock and Snowball managed to get away when the leash slipped out of her hand.

Joe quickly reached to grab Mandie to keep her from falling. "Are you all right?" he asked.

"Yes." She caught her footing as she saw the white cat disappear into the bushes. "Snowball!" She started after him.

"He will not go far in the bushes before his leash will catch and stop him," Dimar told her as he and Joe followed.

But Snowball was experienced at this, and he managed to dodge between bushes and disappear. The cat had cut across the mountainside rather than continue on down the trail they were following.

The three pushed their way through the thicket and followed. Mandie was in the lead, and she suddenly stopped and exclaimed, "Here he is, and look at what he has found!" She stood staring into a clearing.

Joe and Dimar quickly came to her side and gasped in surprise. There ahead of them was one of the missing wagons, and Snowball had jumped up into it. The three rushed forward to investigate.

"Whose wagon is this?" Mandie asked as she reached her white cat, whose leash was now tangled up on a hook in the wagon bed. She got it loose and picked up her cat.

"This wagon belongs to Uncle Wirt," Dimar said, examining the vehicle.

"It doesn't look wrecked or anything," Joe remarked.

Mandie gazed around their surroundings and said, "It's a miracle to me how anyone got it into this space through all those trees."

Dimar quickly went over to one side and pulled at some bushes, which immediately moved, revealing a hidden pathway. "These bushes are not growing here," he said. "Someone put them here to block the way."

Mandie suddenly remembered what they had been doing all this time and asked as she bent to look around, "Are there any footprints here?"

"No, you will not find prints. The thieves made sure to erase all signs," Dimar replied.

"Well, what are we going to do about this wagon?" Joe asked.

"We will leave it here, since we do not have a way to move it," Dimar replied. "And we will look for more wagons and people now that we know they have been here."

Mandie held Snowball, who was trying to get back down into the wagon, and she watched as Dimar shook out a blanket in the wagon bed. Beneath that was a wad of paper that had evidently held food and the cat smelled it. "Snowball, you are a smart cat," she said. "You smelled food and led us right to this wagon."

"But what if there had not been food smells for him to go after?" Joe asked.

"Then we would just chase him until we caught him somewhere," Mandie replied, holding tightly to her cat.

Dimar examined the ground and decided the best thing to do was keep on the trail they had been following. The thieves had covered their own prints, so the three would continue following Uncle Ned's, Sallie's, and Mr. O'Neal's.

"Just think," Mandie said as they walked on. "Uncle Ned must have missed that wagon completely because it is off the trail we are following."

"Perhaps," Dimar said.

"I hope we soon catch up with them," Mandie said with a big sigh. "This has been a pokey day."

Chapter 10 / More Mystery

And it got to be a pokier and pokier day as the three traveled through the mountain. They followed the tracks and markings left by Uncle Ned, Sallie, and Riley O'Neal on several different smaller pathways and then found they looped right back onto the main trail and ended up at the base of the mountain, but not anywhere near where they had started.

"Where are we, Dimar?" Mandie asked, looking around the clearing where they had emerged and holding on to Snowball, who was trying to get down.

"We are near the river," Dimar replied, stooping to look for tracks.

"The river," Joe repeated as he watched Dimar.

"The river," Mandie said, rushing out into the clearing to look around. Suddenly she remembered that she shouldn't be recklessly walking around and perhaps obliterating tracks. She stood still and called back to Dimar, "I'm sorry. I hope I didn't ruin any footprints."

Dimar stood up and smiled at her from a distance as he said, "No, you went the wrong direction. The tracks go this way." He pointed to his right.

Mandie sighed with relief and came back to join the two boys. She and Joe followed as Dimar expertly traced the footprints. She was amazed to see that the tracks led straight to the river when it came into view around a bend.

"Down to the river," Dimar remarked as he led the way, still watching for prints.

The three stood still, staring at the footprints that ended at the riverbank. There were three distinct tracks, belonging to Uncle Ned, Sallie, and Riley O'Neal.

"Well, now what?" Mandie asked, frowning as she looked out over the river.

"There must have been a boat or something here for them to go off on," Joe remarked.

"Yes," Dimar agreed. "They left by boat or raft. I don't think they would have gone swimming out into the water because the current is too swift at this particular place."

"Oh shucks!" Mandie exclaimed, stomping her foot in the sand. "How do we find them now?" She squinted from the glare of the sunshine on the water.

"We survey the river," Dimar said. "We follow the water and watch for markings in the river."

"Markings in the river?" Mandie and Joe both asked at once in surprise.

"Yes, we look for broken twigs on branches that overhang the banks, or anything that is not usual for the river," the Cherokee boy explained.

"Like particles of mica floating in the water maybe?" Mandie asked.

"That is possible. Something caused Uncle Ned to go out on the river," Dimar replied. "We also need to find the place where they left the river."

"Dimar, you are so smart to figure all this out. I would never be able to even start solving this mystery," Mandie told him with a big smile. She tightened her hold on Snowball as he tried to get free.

Dimar bowed his head and wouldn't look at Mandie as he said, "We must begin now. This will take time." He turned to start walking down the bank by the river.

Mandie stayed close behind him and let Snowball down on his leash. Joe followed. They had to walk single file in order to stay close to the river as the banks narrowed to almost nothing in places with trees and bushes growing to the very edge of the water. Dimar stopped to stoop down and examine the ground now and then, but they found no footprints, no broken twigs or any other markings at the water's edge where Uncle Ned could have reached out to mark his path from the boat that he, Sallie, and Riley O'Neal had evidently traveled in.

A long time after they began their search along the river, they rounded a bend and Mandie was the first to exclaim, "I see a boat way down there ahead!" She pointed, then snatched up Snowball who was walking at the end of his leash, and started running toward it.

"Yes, that is a canoe," Dimar agreed and hurried after her.

"But I don't see anyone in it," Joe told them as he, too, raced along the riverbank.

Out of breath, Mandie stopped on the high bank

and looked down at the canoe tied up below in the water.

"Please, do not move around," Dimar cautioned Mandie and Joe as he began searching the ground for prints.

"I'm sure I can see flakes of mica in the boat," Mandie told the boys, pointing to the vessel.

Dimar straightened up to look.

"Yes, so do I," Joe agreed.

"You are right. That is mica in the canoe, tiny flakes," the Cherokee boy added.

Mandie looked down at the ground where they were standing. "Dimar, can you see any footprints?" she asked. Snowball meowed angrily in her arms as he tried to escape.

Dimar pointed to the dirt of the bank going down into the river. "There are tracks coming up this way from the canoe. Then they go into the bushes here," he explained, motioning toward the brush growing nearby. "Now we will follow and see where they go."

Dimar was able to track the prints through the woods, and Mandie found broken twigs along the way, but since she had to carry Snowball, who didn't like it at all, she missed a marking now and then, which Joe was quick to show her.

"You missed one," Joe said with a big grin, pointing to a broken twig.

"Why, Joe, you are getting to be good at this," Mandie teased back.

"It's the company I keep," Joe replied, still grinning.

Soon Dimar led them out of the woods into a clearing. Mandie looked around and was amazed to see Joe's cart and Ned's wagon in the distance, and there were Uncle Ned, Sallie, and Riley O'Neal sitting on the grass by the vehicles.

"Look!" Mandie called out excitedly to the boys as she raced toward the others.

Dimar and Joe quickly followed, and the three plopped down on the ground by their friends, out of breath.

"We waited and y'all never came back," Mandie said, gasping for breath.

"And we tracked you all the way across the mountain, and, mind you, that was quite a job," Joe told them.

"Canoe all we find. We bring it down here," Uncle Ned told them.

"Oh, Uncle Ned, we found Uncle Wirt's wagon," Mandie told him.

"Actually, Snowball found it," Joe corrected her.

"Where?" the old man asked.

Mandie explained where the wagon was and said, "You missed it because it was not on the trail that we went."

"It was covered with bushes," Dimar added.

Uncle Ned looked at the young Cherokee boy and said, "Tonight, we go get wagon."

"Yes, we will get it," Dimar agreed.

"I will go and help," Riley O'Neal told the old man.

"Yes," Uncle Ned agreed.

"Where else are we going to look for the other wagons and the mica?" Mandie asked as she held the end of Snowball's leash while he played in the grass.

"You find wagon in woods. We need look all way in woods there," Uncle Ned replied. He looked up at the sun now low on the horizon. "Late now. We go when sun rise tomorrow."

"It's not really late, Uncle Ned," Mandie protested. "Couldn't we look a little more somewhere else today?"

Uncle Ned looked at Joe and asked, "You go home now?"

Joe frowned as he thought about it and replied, "We don't have to go this very minute, but we do have to be home in time for supper."

"Then we do have a little more time, don't we?" Mandie quickly asked Joe.

"Maybe a little, but not enough time to go back up that mountain. So where else do you want to go?" Joe asked her.

Mandie looked at Sallie and said, "You haven't said a word, Sallie. Do you have any ideas as to where we should look?"

"Since you found Uncle Wirt's wagon up the mountain that we searched, I would think the other two wagons may be in that mountain. But that is too far and takes too long for the rest of today," Sallie replied, glancing at her grandfather.

"Yes, too far," Uncle Ned agreed.

"Do you have any more ideas about who stole the wagons and moved the mica?" Joe asked Uncle Ned.

"Not yet," Uncle Ned replied. "But must be Cherokee."

"I agree," Dimar said.

Uncle Ned stood up. "Now I take Sallie home," he said to Dimar. "Then we get wagon."

Joe also stood up. "And now we go home, Mandie," he said. Looking at Uncle Ned, he asked, "Do you want us to meet you at the Cherokee schoolhouse early tomorrow morning?"

"Yes," the old man said, starting toward his wagon.

Sallie turned to Mandie and said, "School is open tomorrow until noon. I will join you after that."

"And so will I," Riley O'Neal put in. Looking at Uncle Ned, he said, "If you will give us an idea tomorrow morning as to where you are going, Sallie and I will come and join you after we close the school."

"Will go back up same mountain, search woods off trail for other wagons," the old man explained.

"What about the mica, Uncle Ned? Do you think it could have been moved up a mountain?" Mandie asked, picking up Snowball as she rose.

Uncle Ned stopped to look back at her on his way to his wagon. "Not found trail yet for mica but will," he replied. "Soon." He went on to his wagon.

Mandie followed Joe over to his cart as Sallie, Dimar, and Riley O'Neal went to ride with Uncle Ned. They all waved good-bye, and Joe drove toward his house and Uncle Ned toward Deep Creek.

"Do you mind if we go by to see if Mr. Jacob Smith has ever come home?" Mandie asked as they rode down the road.

"Not at all," Joe said with a big smile, looking at Mandie. "That is exactly what I had planned to do. I know you want to see him, but I have become curious as to why we can't find him."

"I am beginning to think that he just went on back to his old house for some reason and that he'll probably get back before I leave," Mandie told him, holding Snowball in her lap. "At least I hope he gets back before Uncle John comes for me."

"Maybe Miss Abigail has some news of him. We'll go by there after we check the house, if he's not home," Joe said, lightly holding the reins as the horse trotted on, pulling the cart.

After a while they came to Mandie's father's house where Mr. Jacob Smith lived. As Joe drove the cart into the yard, he almost ran over a mother hen and a flock of biddies before he saw them. Quickly halting the cart, he jumped down to investigate.

"Joe! Where did they come from?" Mandie asked in surprise as she hurried to join Joe. "You said he doesn't have any chickens."

"He doesn't, at least as of last Friday he didn't," Joe said in a puzzled voice. "I would like to know, too, where they came from."

Mandie watched the chickens roam around the yard after settling down from the fright of the cart. "They act like they belong here," she said, holding tightly to Snowball in her arms as he tried his best to get down.

Joe quickly looked into the barn and said, "He is still gone. His horse is not here," he told Mandie. "Those chickens probably wandered off from their home somewhere and ended up here."

Mandie looked over at the chicken pen by the barn where her father had kept their chickens when he was living here. "I don't suppose Mr. Jacob has anything to feed them, and I don't even see any water anywhere," she said.

Joe glanced back into the barn and said, "No feed around that I can see. When we get back to my house, I can bring something back for them."

"Don't you think we ought to catch them and put them in the pen so someone won't run over them like we almost did?" Mandie asked.

"We can do that when we come back with the feed," Joe said. "Come on. Let's go by Miss Abigail's."

As they got back into the cart and Joe drove it up the path to the main road, Mandie kept watching behind them to be sure they hadn't run over any of the baby chickens or their mama. Memories came back to her of the many chickens her father had raised. He had allowed her to pet the baby ones now and then when the mama wasn't around. She knew the hen would peck her if she caught Mandie handling her brood. And Mandie almost never got used to the idea that someday the babies would grow into full-sized chickens and would sooner or later be made into a meal for the family. She had learned never to get too closely involved with them because of what happened later.

Miss Abigail didn't live very far away, and Joe was soon pulling the cart up by her front door. Mandie jumped down and Joe followed her to the front porch, where the lady was sitting in a rocking chair reading a book in the late afternoon sunshine.

"Come in," Miss Abigail greeted them. "Have a seat." She indicated the swing and other chairs nearby.

"We can't stay, Miss Abigail," Mandie told her as she sat on a chair, still holding Snowball. "We haven't been able to catch up with Mr. Jacob Smith, and we were wondering if you had seen him."

"No, I haven't," Miss Abigail replied, closing her book with a bookmark. "I suppose he must have gone back to his old house for something and got delayed. But it does look like he would let me know because he was supposed to borrow my cart.

Maybe it was an emergency of some kind and he didn't need the cart right then."

Joe sat on the banister and said, "We keep coming by the house and there's still no sign of him returning."

"Oh, Miss Abigail, we just came from there, and there was a hen and a whole bunch of biddies wandering around the yard!" Mandie exclaimed.

"Well, I wonder where they came from?" Miss Abigail said with a frown. "Now, if he hasn't been home all week, those chickens must need feeding."

"We're going to my house to get some feed and bring it back and put them in the chicken pen," Joe told her.

"Now, you all don't have to go all the way back to your house for feed," Miss Abigail objected, rising from the chair. "I have plenty of chicken feed. You just come on back here to the barn with me and get some to take over there, you hear?"

Joe slipped down to his feet and said, "Thank you, Miss Abigail."

Mandie stood up, holding on to Snowball, and followed Miss Abigail and Joe down the steps of the porch and around to the barn in the back. Then she said, "We don't know where the hen and her biddies came from, Miss Abigail. Do you think they belong to someone else and wandered away from their home? Or do you think Mr. Jacob Smith owns them?"

"Oh dear, I just don't know," Miss Abigail said, pausing on the pathway to look back at Mandie. "I do know some of the neighbors were going to sell Mr. Smith some chickens when he got finished moving in. Maybe that's where they came from." She walked on toward the barn.

Mandie and Joe followed. Mandie thought about that and said, "But, Miss Abigail, you said he's still moving things from the old house, and, besides, we haven't seen the chickens there this week and we've been going by every day."

Inside the barn, Miss Abigail handed Joe a sack and told him, "There's plenty of feed over there if you'll just fill this up."

Joe walked over to the corner and found bags of different farm necessities on neat shelves, among which were several containing chicken feed. He quickly filled the empty sack.

"Thank you, Miss Abigail," Joe told her when he had finished. "We'll tell Mr. Smith where we got the feed when we catch up with him."

As they walked back to the front of the house, Mandie remarked, "I'm wondering if there might be more chickens there that we didn't see." Turning to Joe, she said, "We need to search the whole yard. There might be something else that needs to be fed."

"We will," Joe promised. He put the bag of feed into the cart. "Now we'd better hurry and get this done so we won't be late for supper." He jumped up into the cart.

Mandie handed up Snowball to Joe and climbed in after him.

Miss Abigail, standing by the front steps, said, "Will you all please let me know if you find out where Mr. Smith is, or if he returns? This is most peculiar of him to act this way."

"Yes, ma'am," Mandie and Joe said together as he drove the cart back up the road.

When they got back to where Mr. Smith lived,

they found the chickens still roaming around the yard.

"Let's get the feed and water ready first, and then we'll catch them and put them in the pen," Joe said, jumping down from the cart.

Mandie quickly tied Snowball's leash on to a hook in the cart and followed.

Joe drew water from the well and together they washed out the long-unused water trough in the pen. Then they cleaned and dried the containers for the feed.

Mandie happened to look behind her while they were filling the containers with the feed they had brought from Miss Abigail's. The hen had followed them into the pen and was making daring pecks at the feed. "Look, Joe! They are hungry!" she said, straightening up and stepping back so the biddies could follow their mother to the food.

Joe stood by, watching, and said, "The poor things. They are really hungry."

"I'm glad we found them so we could feed them," Mandie said.

Joe edged slowly toward the gate of the pen so as not to disturb the chickens. "Now we'd better get out of here and close them up before they get out again."

Mandie followed him, and as they closed the gate she spied a tiny straggly-looking biddie that had been left behind and was peeping loudly as it ran around the yard. "Look, Joe," she said, slowly moving toward the stray chicken. "Let's pen it in between us and I'll be able to pick it up."

They moved around in a circle and finally Mandie got close enough to snatch up the biddie. It peeped loudly as she quickly took it to the pen and opened the gate to push it through with the others.

"They seem to be tame," Joe remarked.

Mandie watched the stray biddie make its way to the feed trough. "You know, that one looks different. See the black spots on him. He doesn't look like he belongs to the rest of the hen's family."

Joe looked into the pen and said, "You're right, but then sometimes the babies don't all look alike. Let's get going before my mother sends someone to look for us." He laughed, walking toward the cart.

Mandie followed and said, "Your mother wouldn't do that, would she?" She climbed into the vehicle and untied Snowball's leash so she could hold him.

Joe jumped into the cart, picked up the reins, and said, "No, not at my age, I don't think she would, but then, you never know." He drove the cart up to the main road.

"Maybe she knows something about the hen and biddies," Mandie remarked. "Or she might even have some word about Mr. Jacob Smith. Yes, let's do hurry!"

Chapter 11 / Another Search

The next morning was Thursday, and Mandie realized her visit was coming swiftly to an end. Uncle John would be back to get her on Saturday, and she had not really accomplished anything concerning the mysteries she had become involved in. She thought about all this as she dressed and brushed her hair in the guest room at the Woodards.

"Not only have we been unable to solve the mystery concerning the mica and the wagons, but no one knows where Mr. Jacob Smith is," she muttered to herself as she stood before the floor-length mirror. And she quickly added in a loud whisper, "And I haven't even found out what Joe was trying to tell me from the train when he left for college. I ought to go ahead and ask him, I suppose."

When Mandie and Joe had returned to the Woodards' home on the previous afternoon, they found that neither Mrs. Woodard nor Dr. Woodard had heard a word about Mr. Smith. Joe's parents

decided, like Miss Abigail, that the man had returned to his old house for some reason, maybe an
emergency of some kind. They also didn't know
anything about the hen and biddies Mandie and Joe
had found at Mr. Smith's house.

Mandie thought about this as she straightened
her long skirts and went downstairs for breakfast.
Joe was already there waiting for her, and Mrs.
Miller had the food ready. Mrs. Woodard was sleeping late since the doctor had gone out early on calls.
Snowball was hastily eating from a bowl under the
stove.

"Good morning, sleepyhead," Joe greeted her
with a big grin as he stood by the stove watching
Mrs. Miller dish up the food.

"I imagine I was awake before you were. It just
takes a girl longer to dress than it does a boy," Mandie replied, smiling at him and then greeting Mrs.
Miller. "Good morning, Mrs. Miller."

"Good morning, dear," the woman said as she
brought food to the table. "Now y'all hurry up and
eat before everything gets cold. I am packing a basket today for y'all to take with you for your noon
meal."

Mandie and Joe hurried to the table and sat
down. Mrs. Miller poured coffee for them.

"Thanks for remembering to give us food to
take with us today," Joe told her as he passed the
platter of scrambled eggs to Mandie.

"You shouldn't go around eating other folks'
cooking. You never know how clean it is," Mrs.
Miller told him as she took down a basket from a
shelf.

Mandie looked at her quickly and said, "Mrs.
Miller, our friends shared their food with us. I have

been in their houses and they are just as clean as we are."

Mrs. Miller's face turned red and she became flustered as she packed biscuits into the basket. "Why, I didn't mean your friends at all. I am packing enough that you can share your food with them today."

"Thank you, Mrs. Miller," Joe said. Turning to Mandie, he said, "Guess we'd better hurry so we won't keep Uncle Ned and the others waiting." He began eating the food he had piled onto his plate.

"Yes," Mandie agreed and started in on her food. "I suppose Uncle Ned and Dimar were able to get Uncle Wirt's wagon down from the mountain last night. And I'm thinking, since it couldn't possibly come down the narrow trail we traveled yesterday, they would have had to go in a different direction. There must be other wider paths in that mountain. And just maybe they found the other two wagons on their way down."

"Maybe," Joe agreed. "Remember Uncle Ned said they were going to search the whole mountain?"

"I remember," Mandie answered. "My time is getting short, and I want to hurry up and solve all these mysteries before I have to go home."

"And before I have to return to college," Joe reminded her.

"I suppose Uncle Ned will keep on searching for the wagons and the mica if we don't find it before we leave," Mandie remarked, quickly sipping her coffee. Then looking at Joe she said with a big smile, "I'll be ready to go as soon as you are."

After they finished their food, Mandie put the leash on Snowball and picked him up. Joe got his rifle and took the basket of food from Mrs. Miller. They got into Mrs. Woodard's cart and hurried down the road to the Cherokee schoolhouse.

Uncle Ned and Dimar were already there, talking to Sallie and Riley O'Neal in the doorway of the schoolhouse. Mandie looked inside and saw six Cherokee children sitting at desks. She had let Snowball walk on his leash and he tried to go inside.

Uncle Ned was busy explaining to his granddaughter where they were going so that she and Riley could catch up with them when the school closed. Sallie knew the territory but Riley O'Neal didn't.

"We will find you," Sallie called to them as Dimar left his horse tied up under a tree and followed Uncle Ned and got in his wagon. Mandie and Joe got back in the cart. Mandie held the white cat in her lap.

"We go other side of mountain today where we brought down Wirt's wagon," the old man explained. He and Dimar had not taken time to look for the other wagons the night before because it was late by the time they had found a way to get the wagon down.

Mandie and Joe followed the old man and Dimar, and they ended up at the foot of the same mountain but in a different place from where they had been yesterday. Uncle Ned pulled his wagon under a shade tree, and he and Dimar jumped down. Joe stopped the cart nearby, and he and Mandie joined them. Snowball insisted on getting down, so Mandie let him walk at the end of his leash.

Suddenly Mandie remembered Mr. Jacob Smith. "Uncle Ned, we didn't ask if you or Dimar had seen Mr. Jacob Smith anywhere yesterday. He's still not home," Mandie explained as the four of them stood by the wagon and cart.

Uncle Ned shook his head, "No, have not seen him."

Dimar also said, "No, I have not."

Mandie told them about finding the hen and biddies in Jacob Smith's yard. "Do y'all know of anyone who would have brought the chickens to his house and left them?" she asked.

Uncle Ned and Dimar both shook their heads.

"Maybe chickens lost," the old man suggested, taking his bow and arrows from his wagon.

Dimar was carrying a rifle again, and he shouldered that, ready to go up the mountain.

"Now we go," Uncle Ned told them, walking toward a trail beyond the wagon.

Mandie picked up Snowball and quickly caught up with him and asked, "Are we all staying together today? We're not going to split up like we did yesterday, are we?"

Uncle Ned looked down at her and smiled. "We stay together. Quicker." He walked on and the others followed him.

The trail was not as steep as the one they had traveled yesterday, but it completely disappeared in places and they had to fight their way through bushes and underbrush. Uncle Ned was very thorough and went slow enough to examine smaller pathways on the side from time to time.

Joe walked directly behind the old man and Mandie followed him. Dimar brought up the rear with his rifle. Sometimes Mandie allowed Snowball to walk and sometimes she carried him. She had trouble with him trying to chase after everything that moved in the bushes—squirrels, birds, chipmunks, and unseen inhabitants of the woods.

"I could carry Snowball for a while," Joe offered as he looked back to see Mandie quickly pulling on the leash to keep Snowball from getting away.

"Thank you, Joe, but you have your rifle. Besides, you need to be free to use it if we run into any trouble," Mandie replied, picking up the white cat and holding him on her shoulder.

"Joe could carry Snowball and I could shoot my rifle if we have trouble," Dimar said with a big smile.

"No, no. I thank you both, but I'll manage," she said as they walked on.

Mandie noticed that Uncle Ned was not leading them straight to the top of the mountain but was more or less circling around it at various intervals. At some places they had to walk on a steep incline, with one foot higher than the other, but by speaking firmly to her cat she was able to control him.

Then they came to the place where Uncle Wirt's wagon had been hidden. Uncle Ned and Dimar had removed the bushes hiding it, and Mandie saw that it was a good-sized clearing with a path leading out of the other side from where they were.

"Now we rest," Uncle Ned said, walking into the clearing and pointing toward a small waterfall coming out of the side of the mountain. "Water." He went to it, cupped his hands, and drank.

The others followed, doing likewise. Mandie let Snowball down to drink from the rocks where the water fell. Then they all sat on the grass and relaxed.

"Whew!" Mandie exclaimed. "Feels good to sit down. Uncle Ned, is there a lot more of this mountain to search? Are we almost finished?"

The old man replied, "Top." He pointed upward.

"Few minutes, then go down to wagon. Eat."

"Eat, that's a magic word," Joe said with a big grin.

Mandie looked at Dimar and said, "You know something? We brought loads of food with us today."

Dimar smiled and said, "Do not need a load, only a little. Too much food will make us lazy."

"But I need food for strength," Joe teased. "You are used to climbing all over mountains, and I've been citified all this year without a chance to exercise, like following Mandie around on her mysteries." He turned to grin at Mandie.

"Just think, you only have two more days to follow me, really one day, because Uncle John will be coming for me on Saturday," Mandie replied, smiling.

Uncle Ned stood up and said, "We go now. Make haste."

The three followed the old man to the top of the mountain and then all the way back down to the wagon and the cart without finding any clues whatsoever to the missing wagons or the mica. They were all tired and disgusted.

But when the food was spread out on a blanket in the grass, Mandie saw that Uncle Ned had brought lots of fried chicken, Dimar had brought many biscuits filled with meat, and Mrs. Miller had given her and Joe ham biscuits and chocolate cake. Besides all this food, there was plenty of milk and coffee to drink.

"Shucks, we can't eat all that food and then travel up another mountain," Mandie said, laughing as she tied Snowball's leash to the wheel of the cart.

"Not another mountain," Uncle Ned told her as

he reached for food to fill one of the tin plates he had brought. "We search valley, river, cornfields, cave."

"Cave?" Mandie quickly asked in surprise and almost choked on a bite of ham biscuit she was chewing. "A cave? We're going to a cave?"

Joe also stopped eating to listen, but Dimar, knowing the territory, sat there smiling as Uncle Ned explained.

"Big cave across valley under mountain," Uncle Ned said. "We go in it."

"But, Mandie, you remember that cave we went in and it collapsed?" Joe asked her. "Do you want to go into another cave?"

"Well, if Uncle Ned says it's safe," she replied slowly, looking at the old man.

Uncle Ned nodded and said, "Many hundred years old. Cave safe."

"It is safe, Mandie," Dimar told her. "I have been in it many times."

"If y'all say so," Joe managed to say with his mouth full of fried chicken.

"Yes, if y'all think it's safe, then it must be safe. Let's hurry and go there," she said, quickly digging into her food.

They finished the meal and repacked the various utensils and leftovers. Uncle Ned and Joe took their horses to a nearby waterfall to drink and then retied them in the shade where they could eat grass.

"We ready now," Uncle Ned said, pulling three lanterns out of his wagon. He handed one to Joe and one to Dimar and kept the third one.

Mandie picked up Snowball and asked, "Don't I get a lantern, Uncle Ned? Suppose I get lost from y'all in the cave. I wouldn't have a light."

Uncle Ned smiled and said, "No, Papoose, you

got cat. No need for lantern. We go together."

"Uncle Ned, I was thinking about Sallie and Mr. O'Neal," Mandie said as they started to follow the old man. "Do you think they will find us?"

"School may be late, but they find us later," Uncle Ned replied. "I tell Sallie where we go."

They traveled across the valley, pausing only to search behind clumps of bushes and trees here and there. Then Uncle Ned led the way through a dense forest to a cluster of huge boulders that seemed to be the base of the mountain. Uncle Ned and Dimar set down their lanterns, rifle, and bow and arrows, and walked right up to the stones and began pushing on a large one.

"Here, let me help!" Joe quickly lay his rifle down beside Mandie and handed her the lantern he was carrying, then ran to assist them.

Evidently the stones were not as heavy as they looked, because the large one rolled to one side and uncovered the mouth of a cave. Mandie watched in fascination. She had seen caves before, at least two of them, but had never seen one closed up with a boulder for a door.

Uncle Ned and Dimar stepped back and picked up their things while Joe retrieved his rifle and lantern.

"Now we go in. Must stay together. Must. Remember that," he said as he bent to light his lantern.

Dimar did the same with his lantern. Joe, watching, quickly struck a match to his lantern also.

"But, Uncle Ned, why was the boulder in front of the door to the cave?" Mandie asked as the old man motioned for her to walk directly behind him.

"Keep out animals, hide cave from other people," Uncle Ned explained. "Now we go." He continued into the cave with Mandie right behind him.

Even with the lanterns, the inside of the cave looked spooky. Snowball didn't seem to like the place and tried to scratch Mandie in an effort to get down. She quickly scolded him, and he clung to the shoulder of her dress.

The entrance was like a long hallway, not very wide and with a low ceiling. As they continued, Mandie was amazed to find they were coming into another part that had several large rooms opening off the hallway. From what she could see, the place was furnished with enough necessities, such as beds, dishes, water pails, blankets, and quilts, that it could be lived in.

"Does someone live here, Uncle Ned?" she asked, finding that her voice echoed as she tried to lower it.

"Now and then," the old man said. "For special people, special times. Old days Cherokee people hide here from white people when white people take our land and make us move." He stopped to look at her.

"But your people never lived here, did they? My great-grandfather Shaw built that tunnel in the house where Uncle John lives now to hide your people until all those horrible things were over," Mandie reminded him.

"My people all live in house of your great-grandfather in tunnel. Your great-grandfather man of God, loved all people," Uncle Ned said with sadness in his voice.

Mandie reached forward to squeeze his old wrinkled hand as they continued into the cave.

They examined the whole place. Uncle Ned inspected the dishes and blankets and then decided that no one had been in the cave. He turned to lead the way out. When they almost reached the entrance to go outside, Mandie suddenly heard Sallie calling to Uncle Ned.

"My grandfather!" she was saying from outside the cave. "Are you in the cave, my grandfather?"

"Yes, my granddaughter," Uncle Ned called back as they reached the exit.

Sallie and Mr. O'Neal were standing there, waiting for them.

"Oh, Sallie, I'm so glad you caught up with us," Mandie told her friend as she let Snowball down to walk.

"I am glad, too," Sallie replied. Looking at her grandfather, she asked, "Have you found anything yet?"

"Not yet, but we will," Uncle Ned told her as he extinguished his lantern.

"Then we are not too late to help a little," Riley O'Neal told him.

Uncle Ned nodded and pointed across the valley. "We go now, across cornfields," he said.

Dimar and Joe put out their lanterns, and everyone started across the clearing. To Mandie it looked two miles wide, and Snowball was really heavy, but he would slow things up if she let him walk.

As though Sallie had read her mind, the girl held her arms out and said, "Let me carry Mr. Snowball. He is heavy, and you have been carrying him all day."

"All right, for a little while," Mandie agreed and handed over the white cat. Snowball knew Sallie and didn't cause any trouble.

They followed Uncle Ned across the huge corn-

fields and out onto another road. There was no sign
of anyone anywhere. They passed an old barn and
later a shack, but didn't see a living soul. Finally
Uncle Ned paused on the road.

"We go two more miles, then we turn off toward
wagon and cart," he said. He looked up at the sky
and said, "Getting late."

"Oh shucks!" Mandie exclaimed. "If we don't
find anything or anybody within the next two miles,
then we have to quit, and I only have one whole day
left to help."

Uncle Ned smiled at her and said, "Maybe we
find wagons. Maybe we find mica. We look two more
miles for them."

They walked the two additional miles and still
didn't see anyone. Then Uncle Ned turned left at the
intersection of another road. A small country
church stood there with a small cemetery walled in
around it.

Mandie had taken Snowball back from Sallie
and was letting him walk at the end of his leash
since they were on a smooth road. He suddenly decided he wanted to run away and managed to jerk
the leash out of Mandie's hand. She raced after him
down the road toward the corner where the church
stood. He slowed down now and then to see if his
mistress was following, then he ran on. This was an
old game with him.

Everyone also walked faster to try to help catch
the cat. Mandie chased him right up to the iron gate
in the wall where he had to slow down, and she
managed to capture him.

"I got him!" she called out to her friends as she
held him tightly in her arms. As she turned around
to look back at her friends, something in the cem-

etery sparkled and caught her attention. She gasped in disbelief as she stared through the iron gate. There was all that mica, spread all over the cemetery.

"I can't believe it!" she screamed, and everyone came running to see.

"There is the mica!" Joe said, excitedly grasping the rods in the gate.

Uncle Ned and the others stood staring, too, with various exclamations.

Mandie quickly grasped Uncle Ned's hand as tears formed in her blue eyes. "Uncle Ned, how could anyone do this?"

Uncle Ned patted her blond head and said, "We find who did this. Take time, but we find."

"I would like to find them myself," Mandie said, angrily wiping a tear from her eye. "We have to clean it all off, Uncle Ned."

"We go home now. Come back tomorrow, clean mica away," the old man said.

Mandie jerked on his hand as she said, "Not tomorrow, Uncle Ned. We need to clean it all off today. Today, Uncle Ned!"

Uncle Ned looked down at her and said, "No tools. No way to get it out. Must come back tomorrow with tools."

Mandie stomped her feet and said, "No, no, Uncle Ned! We can go right now and get some tools and get it all out. Oh, it's horrible to do such a thing to graves."

Uncle Ned was silent a moment and no one else said anything. Then he said, "All right, Papoose. We go get wagon, get tools, and come back today."

Mandie smiled through her tears and said, "Thank you, Uncle Ned."

She knew this was going to be a big job and would take time, but she also knew she wouldn't sleep that night knowing all those graves were buried under all that mica. She silently thanked God that He had persuaded Uncle Ned to return and remove it today.

Chapter 12 / The Message

As Uncle Ned promised, they went back and got his wagon and Joe's cart, then they went to the Cherokee schoolhouse, where Riley O'Neal gave them tools to remove the mica. Riley and Dimar rode their own horses back with them, because it would be late when they finished the job and everyone could just go on home without someone having to go out of their way to drop someone off.

When they entered the cemetery, Mandie looked around and asked Uncle Ned, "Where are we going to put all this mica when we take it out of here?"

"Old barn back there behind wall. We throw it all by barn and take it away later," Uncle Ned replied.

"Take it away? Where?" Mandie asked.

"Must belong to mica mine somewhere. We find," Uncle Ned told her.

So they began the huge task of loading Uncle Ned's wagon and then Joe's cart with the mica and then dumping it out by the old barn.

As she shoveled the mica, Mandie wandered back into the far corner of the cemetery, looking at gravestones, when she thought she heard one of her friends say something. But they were all at the other end of the cemetery, so she called to them, "What did you say?"

Everyone looked at her in surprise and said, "Nothing."

Mandie thought they didn't understand what she said, so she went back to work shoveling the mica into a pile when she definitely heard someone crying, "Help!" in a muffled voice. She quickly walked around and looked, but couldn't see anyone else near her. She stopped by a six-foot-tall monument with an angel on top and tried to figure out what was going on.

"Help!" came from the monument, and she got goosebumps for a moment as she thought the angel had spoken. She quickly moved back, and when she did she saw a man's face looking up at her from under the bench part of the monument. He was covered entirely with the mica except his face, and evidently he was alive.

Mandie's heart almost stopped beating as she imagined all kinds of things, from thinking she had imagined it to believing someone in a grave had come back alive. Then Joe came rushing up to join her. She was so frightened she couldn't speak, but pointed toward the monument.

"What is it, Mandie?" Joe asked, looking at her and then to where she was pointing. He immediately saw the man's face and fell on his knees to start uncovering the man. "Come on, Mandie! Help me."

Mandie finally realized what was going on, and

she joined Joe in his effort to dig the man out of the mica. When they had removed enough mica that the man could sit up, Mandie gasped in surprise. "Oh, it's Mr. Beethoven! Mr. Beethoven, how did you get buried?" She reached to brush the mica out of his hair.

The others had come running when they saw what was going on, and they soon had Mr. Beethoven out of the mess of mica. The man remembered seeing them in the mountain and tried to thank them, but he could hardly speak.

"Water," Uncle Ned told Dimar, who rushed back to the wagon to get Uncle Ned's water jug.

Uncle Ned helped Beethoven move away from the pile of mica, and when he did the old Indian spied an arrow under where the man had been buried. He picked it up and muttered, "Tsa'ni!"

Mandie and the others heard the name. "Tsa'ni? Did he do this, Uncle Ned?" Tsa'ni was a young Cherokee boy who hated white people, and everyone knew him for his bad deeds.

Uncle Ned nodded as he still examined the arrow and said, "Arrow belong to Tsa'ni."

"What are we going to do about it?" Joe asked.

"I tell Council," Uncle Ned said. "Council do something."

"I'm glad he won't get away with doing all this," Mandie said. "Why, he could have killed Mr. Beethoven here."

Dimar had returned with the water, and Beethoven slowly drank from the jug. He finally regained his voice. "I had been walking a long time and decided to take a nap in here. With the wall around the cemetery, no wild animals could get in, so I thought I was safe. I lay down in the shade under that monument and went to sleep. When I woke up, I couldn't move. I was covered all over with that mica, but the bench part of the monument had shielded my face," he told them.

"But who dumped the mica on you? Why didn't you run away?" Joe asked.

Beethoven shook his head and said, "I don't know who did it. I was asleep."

"Arrow say Tsa'ni did it," Uncle Ned said firmly. He handed the arrow to Dimar and said, "Put arrow in safe place under seat in wagon. Now we finish moving mica."

Dimar did as Uncle Ned said and then hurried back to help load more mica. When they had the wagon and the cart full, Dimar drove the wagon and Joe the cart toward the old barn outside the wall of the cemetery.

Joe was ahead of Dimar and couldn't decide where the best place was to dump the mica, so he started to circle the old barn and look around. He drew the horse up short suddenly, almost causing Dimar to run his wagon into the back of the cart. With the heavy mica, it was hard to stop the vehicles.

Glancing quickly back at Dimar, he yelled, "Look!" He pointed ahead. "There are the two missing wagons." Joe jumped down to investigate, and Dimar hurried to join him.

"Yes," Dimar agreed with a big smile. "My mother's wagon and Jessan's wagon." He examined the vehicles.

Joe quickly looked in the bed of each one. There were definitely mica particles in both.

Mandie had been near the gate when the two boys drove their loads out, and she stepped outside to see where they had gone. When she saw the two vehicles standing there in the field, she wondered where Dimar and Joe had gone and hurried to investigate.

"Joe! Dimar!" she called as she came closer. "Where are y'all?" Then as she rounded the corner of the barn, she saw the boys with the two missing wagons. She rushed over to look.

"Here are the two wagons we've been searching all over the mountain for," Joe told her with a big grin.

"Of all places!" she exclaimed. She looked at the barn and asked, "Have y'all looked in the barn? There might be something else hidden in there that was stolen." She started for the door, which was barely handing on its hinges.

"Here, wait, I'll open that. It might fall off on you," Joe told her. He and Dimar carefully swung the door back, and the three of them entered the dark interior of the barn and were greeted by a strange snoring sound.

Mandie froze in her tracks. "What was that?" she asked.

"I do believe it's a horse," Joe said, going toward a stall at the end of the corridor. "That's what it is," he immediately called back.

Dimar and Mandie followed him. In the dim light coming through cracks in the wooden wall of the barn, Mandie could see the horse. Then she also spotted something else lying on the floor and almost screamed as she backed away.

"No!" she cried.

Joe and Dimar quickly investigated the floor.

"It's a man all tied up and gagged!" Joe told her.

"Run and get the water jug out of my cart! It's under the seat."

Mandie raced outside, grabbed the jug from under the seat, and returned, holding it out to Joe, who was stooping over the man.

"Mandie, set the water down a minute. You don't have to be afraid," Joe told her. "It's Mr. Jacob Smith!"

"Yes," Dimar confirmed as the two boys worked quickly to remove the ropes and the gag in Mr. Smith's mouth.

Mandie watched, and as soon as they got the gag out of the man's mouth, he tried to speak. She grabbed the water and held it up to his mouth. He drank and then spluttered as he tried to talk.

When the young people were gone too long, the others came to look for them and hurried across the field to the two loaded vehicles, then into the barn.

Uncle Ned was the first one inside, and he looked at Mr. Jacob Smith as the boys finished untying him and asked, "Who did this?" He knelt by the man who was now sitting up.

Jacob Smith shook his head and mumbled in a dry voice, "Don't know them. All Cherokee boys."

"Tsa'ni!" Uncle Ned said angrily. "Council will take care of him. I find other boys and Council will take care of them, too."

"Let's get the wagon unloaded so we can put Mr. Smith in it and get him out of here," Riley told the boys.

With everyone pitching in, it didn't take but a few minutes to clean the wagon out and then the cart. They got Mr. Smith into the wagon and drove the vehicles back to the gate of the cemetery.

"I will water the horse, Mr. Smith," Dimar told

him. "There is a creek down the hill behind that barn." He hurried back to do this.

Mandie excitedly asked questions as soon as Mr. Smith was able to talk. "How long have you been in that barn? We've been going by your house looking for you every day this week," she told him as he lay against the side in the bed of the wagon and she and Joe knelt nearby.

"I had to go back to my old house," Mr. Smith said between gasps for breath. "Got word someone wanted to rent it. Went up there last Saturday, I think it was. Came back down this road yesterday and caught those boys throwing mica all over the cemetery." He paused to lick his lips and swallow a little water. "Told them if they didn't stop, I was going to find someone who would stop them. They overpowered me. More of them than I thought." He stopped to breathe.

Uncle Ned had been listening as he stood beside the wagon. He told Mandie, "Must go now. Take Mr. Smith and other man home to Morning Star. She doctor."

"I'm all right. I can go on to my house," Mr. Smith insisted, but he fell back against the side of the wagon and gasped for breath.

"No, we go home to Morning Star," the old Cherokee man insisted. Turning to Dimar, he said, "We get other man in wagon." Then looking at Mandie, he said, "I promise we come back tomorrow, finish moving mica. Must take sick men home now."

"I understand, Uncle Ned," Mandie replied. "That's the right thing to do."

Dimar came back with Riley O'Neal, the two of them almost carrying Beethoven to the wagon.

They lifted him and set him beside Mr. Smith.

Mandie looked at Mr. Smith and explained, "This man was buried alive under all that mica in the cemetery."

"You don't say!" Mr. Smith said in surprise as he looked at Beethoven.

Beethoven was trying to resist being put into the wagon and tried to get out, but was too weak to do that. "Got to git to Georgia. Got to git a job," he kept muttering.

Mandie quickly explained to Mr. Smith who Beethoven was and how they had met him.

Mr. Smith looked at Beethoven, reached out his hand to shake hands, and said, "Man, you done got a job. I need someone to help me real bad."

"But I ain't got to Georgia yet," Beethoven argued.

"You're almost to Georgia. Anyhow, you got a job," Mr. Smith said, still offering his hand.

Evidently Beethoven was woozy from his ordeal, and he waved his right hand out and managed to connect with Mr. Smith's. "I thank you, mister. I thank you," he said and stopped trying to get out of the wagon.

Uncle Ned told Dimar, "We tie Mr. Smith's horse behind wagon. You ride yours. We don't leave horse here. We come back for two wagons."

Joe rushed around, gathering up the tools and putting them in the back of Uncle Ned's wagon. Mandie and Sallie helped, and they were all soon ready to go.

"Mr. Smith, I have to go home Saturday," Mandie called to him as Uncle Ned got ready to drive away with the wagon. "If you're able, will you come to see me?"

"That I will," Mr. Smith answered as she jumped into Joe's cart, untied Snowball from the hook where she had left him, and Joe started down the road.

Mandie took a long breath and said, "Oh, I think I'm tired!"

"I know I'm tired, and I know I'm hungry and my mother will be wondering where we are," Joe told her as he shook the reins.

They were late for supper, but Dr. and Mrs. Woodard had gone to a friend's house for supper and left Mrs. Miller to serve the two young people. When Mandie and Joe walked in the back door, Mrs. Miller turned from the stove, where she was inspecting the contents of a pot. Her eyes widened and she exclaimed, "For pity sakes, what happened to y'all?"

Mandie and Joe both laughed then as they realized they must have mica particles all over their clothes.

"It's a long story, but first we need to get cleaned up, if you don't mind holding supper a few minutes more," Joe told her as he smiled and headed for the door to the hallway.

"No rush. Your ma and pa ain't here anyhow," Mrs. Miller replied. "They've gone to the Thompsons' for supper. I suppose you don't know because you didn't see them this morning."

"That's fine. At least we didn't hold up their supper," Joe replied.

"I'll be right back down as soon as I can get rid of all this mica," Mandie said with a laugh as she followed Joe out the door.

When they came back downstairs, cleaned up for supper, the two related the events of the day to

Mrs. Miller, who probably didn't believe everything they told her.

"Uh-huh," Mrs. Miller kept saying, glancing at Mandie and then at Joe as she served the food. "Uh-huh."

"I know all this is hard to believe, but it really and truly happened," Mandie told her.

"You don't say," Mrs. Miller muttered.

Mandie whispered to Joe, "No use telling her anything. She doesn't believe us."

"I know," Joe whispered back, and then raising his voice he said, "Let's take our coffee and sit in the parlor when we finish."

"Of course," Mandie replied with a grin.

When Joe's parents came home that night and found them in the parlor, Mrs. Woodard immediately told them she would expect them to stay home the next day because she had not had any time with them and also friends had been by and missed them.

So the next day was taken up with people dropping in to say hello and with Mrs. Woodard keeping a table filled with food all day long.

Then the next day was Saturday. When Mandie got up that morning, she knew Uncle John would be coming to get her and she still hadn't had a chance to talk to Mr. Jacob Smith. She also knew all her friends had been working on the mica the day before and had been too busy to come by.

But Saturday was different. The first thing that morning, Uncle Ned and Sallie arrived, bringing Riley O'Neal with them. They reported that Mr. Jacob Smith had been able to go home the day before, taking Beethoven Jones with him. Then Mr.

Smith himself, with Beethoven Jones in tow, showed up.

"Oh, Mr. Smith, I'm so glad you and Mr. Beethoven are recovered and came by to see me," Mandie told them as everyone gathered in the long kitchen where Mrs. Woodard had had Mrs. Miller set out a table full of food.

"And we're glad of that, too," Mr. Smith said, his eyes lighting up with a smile.

"I wanted to ask you something," Mandie began. "Do you happen to know whether my father's rifle was still in the house when you moved in?"

"I sure do," Mr. Smith said. "It's hanging right over the door where he always kept it. I've been keeping it cleaned and oiled. I knew you would want it someday."

With tears in her blue eyes, Mandie reached to squeeze his hand and said, "Thank you, Mr. Jacob." She took a breath and added, "Would you keep it for me? I'll get it one day, but I'll know it's safe with you."

"That I will," he said, squeezing her hand back.

Joe was seated nearby and said, "I heard someone else drive up outside." He went to look out the window and turned back to Mandie. "It's your uncle John, and guess who's with him?"

Mandie looked at him in surprise and asked, "Who?"

Joe grinned and said, "Your grandmother, Mrs. Taft."

"Grandmother?" Mandie repeated, and then sighing, she added, "And I know why she came. She wants to talk you into traveling this summer."

Joe went to open the door. Dr. Woodard had also

seen them and came across the room to greet them with Joe.

"Come in, come in," Dr. Woodard told them.

"Howdy," John Shaw said, stepping into the kitchen as he helped Mrs. Taft through the door.

"Grandmother, how did you get with Uncle John?" Mandie asked. It had just dawned on her that she had left her grandmother at Uncle John's house, but Uncle John had been in Asheville on business all this time, or was supposed to be.

As Mrs. Woodard came into the room and went to greet the new arrivals, Mrs. Taft explained, "He was in Asheville, so I decided to go on home to Asheville. Then he came by the house and asked if I would like to come with him to bring you home."

"I'm so glad you could come," Mrs. Woodard told her, and the two women went on into the hallway.

"Why did Uncle John do that?" Mandie whispered under her breath to Joe.

Later that day Mandie found that they weren't going to be leaving until the next day, Sunday. All her friends left in the afternoon and that night she, Uncle John, and her grandmother sat in the parlor with the Woodards, talking about nothing in particular.

Then suddenly Mrs. Taft looked directly at Joe and asked, "Would you like to come along on a vacation trip with Amanda and me this summer?"

Joe quickly replied, "I'm sorry, Mrs. Taft, but I'm not sure I'll be having any vacation time away from school. You see, I might have to go to school all summer to catch up enough to become a full college student in the fall."

"But the school will most likely give you some

breaks over the whole summer, won't they?" she asked.

"I don't know for sure right now," Joe told her.

"Well, Amanda, Celia's mother has given permission for Celia to travel with us on a vacation to wherever you want to go," Mrs. Taft told Mandie.

"But, Grandmother, I had already told you I wanted to visit with my friends, all of us going from one house to the other, remember?" Mandie replied.

"But that won't take all summer, Amanda," Mrs. Taft said. "I'll tell you what I had in mind. Remember Senator Morton from our journey to Europe? He has invited us to visit him at his home in Florida, and you know I can't very well go to a man's home by myself. But if you would come along, we could also bring Celia and it would all be nice and proper. What do you say, dear?"

Mandie took a deep breath and was at a loss for words. She looked at Joe who kept a solemn face. She glanced around the room. Everyone seemed to be looking at her and waiting for her reply.

Finally Mandie turned to Joe and asked, "Are you sure you have to go to school all summer?"

"Mandie, I told you I was not sure, but I do know I will have to attend a class for the first two weeks of vacation. I know I won't be home before then," Joe told her. "And if I do come home, I thought we'd be visiting with our friends."

Mandie looked at her grandmother and asked, "When are you planning to visit Senator Morton?"

"Well, plans are flexible. After hearing that Joe will definitely be tied up the first two weeks of vacation, I'm sure you and Celia and I could go then," Mrs. Taft replied. "That way you'd be back home by the time Joe gets home, and you and your friends could visit as you wanted."

Mandie looked at Joe again and then back at Mrs. Taft as she slowly replied, "All right, Grandmother. I'll go for those two weeks."

"Thank you, dear," Mrs. Taft said with a big smile. "I'm sure you will enjoy Florida because you've never been there."

The adults got involved in their own conversation then, and Mandie stood up and motioned to Joe. "Let's go out on the porch," she said.

Joe silently followed and they went to sit in rocking chairs on the long front porch. The air was cool but not really cold and it was very dark.

Mandie had decided it was now or never. She had to ask Joe what he had been yelling back to her from the train that day in Franklin when he had left for college.

They were both silent for a few moments and then Joe said, "I suppose we need to write to Jonathan in New York and find out when he's getting out of school so we can at least make some plans to get together."

"But how can we make plans when you don't know whether you'll even be home or not?" Mandie asked.

"Just make the plans, and if I get home I'll join in. Otherwise, the rest of you can get together," Joe told her.

"I don't think I like the uncertain schedules of colleges if they're all like yours," Mandie said.

"But, Mandie, this is just a special case because I didn't have all the requirements to get in full time. I've explained all that to you before," Joe reminded her.

"Speaking of colleges," Mandie began slowly, glancing at him out of the corner of her eye. "Remember that day you left Franklin to go to college?"

"I sure do," Joe said with a little laugh. "The happiest day of my life."

"Do you also remember that you were yelling something out the train window when it pulled out of the station. I couldn't understand what you said, except that you said you'd write and you never did write. All I ever got from you was that note saying you'd be home for the spring holidays," she quickly finished.

Joe leaned forward to look at her and said, "But that was it. That note. I was trying to tell you I might be able to come home for the spring break. I did write and let you know."

Mandie couldn't believe her ears. She took a deep, deep breath and said, "Oh shucks!"

Look for Mandie Book 32, *Mandie and the Seaside Rendezvous*, to be published in October 1999. "The strange woman" whom Mandie and Celia encountered on their European travels will appear again in St. Augustine, Florida!

Great Gifts for MANDIE

The ***MANDIE Datebook*** is a reminder of birthdays and other important dates. Highlights occasions Mandie holds dear! Hardcover.

The ***MANDIE Diary*** is a perfect place to write special thoughts. Features a brass lock and key! Hardcover.

SNOWBALL Stationery is the purr-fect way to write letters to friends—or fan letters to author Lois Gladys Leppard! Timesaving tri-fold stationery includes self-adhesive stickers to seal notes-no envelopes needed. Set of 12 notes and stickers.

fans!

SNOWBALL®, Mandie's constant companion and loyal friend, can now be yours! This adorable 5" tall, plush bean bag toy has soft "long-hair" fur, blue gem eyes, and a name tag collar.

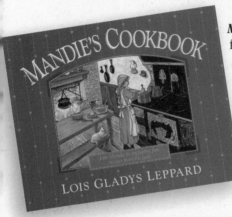

MANDIE'S *Cookbook* is filled with Mandie's favorite recipes as well as the fascinating experiences of girls from the turn of the century. Spiral Binding.

Available from your nearest Christian bookstore (800) 991-7747 or from Bethany House Publishers.

The Leader in Christian Fiction!

BETHANY  HOUSE PUBLISHERS

11400 Hampshire Ave. South
Minneapolis, MN 55438

www.bethanyhouse.com

Are you a member of the Mandie® fan club?
If not, write,

Mandie® Fan Club
Post Office Box 5945
Greenville, South Carolina 29606